THE USBORNE
BOOK OF
LONDON

Moira Butterfield
Designed by Sue Mims

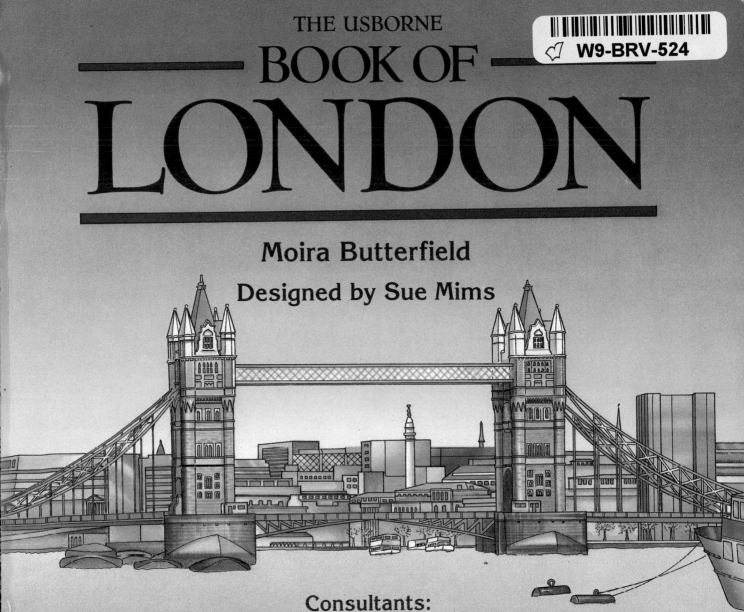

Consultants:
Leon Preston, member of the Guild of Guide Lecturers
Geoffrey Toms, Museum of London Education Officer

Editor: Tony Potter

Illustrated by: Joe McEwan, Ian Jackson, Terence Dalley,
Guy Smith, Kim Blundell

Additional illustrations by Peter Bull, Brenda Haw, Martin Newton

Cover illustration by Kate Davies, Chris West

Photography by Chris Gilbert

W9-BRV-524

Contents

First published in 1987 by Usborne Publishing Ltd, 83-85 Saffron Hill, London EC1N 8RT, England.

Copyright © 1993, 1987 Usborne Publishing Ltd.

The name Usborne and the device 🜛 are trade Marks of Usborne Publishing Ltd. All rights reserved.

No part of this publication may be reproduced, stored in a retrieval system or transmitted in any form or by any means, electronic, mechanical, photocopying, recording or otherwise, without the prior permission of the publisher.

Printed in Great Britain

U.E.

About this book

London, the capital of Great Britain, is the biggest city in the country, with a population of nearly seven million people. It has developed over nearly 2,000 years, and many of its streets and buildings have amazing stories and events connected with them.

This book gives you a taste of London's past, and of its life today, with a detailed look at its history, its major buildings and events.

Some of the London characters in this book.

First there is an introduction to London's history, from the time of the very first Roman settlers up to the twentieth century. You can find out why London has grown and about some of its famous characters of the past, both real and fictional. These include Samuel Pepys, who wrote a seventeenth century diary, Charles Dickens, who chronicled Victorian London in his novels, the fictional detective Sherlock Holmes and Dick Whittington, who was three times Lord Mayor.

There is lots of information about the most famous sites in London – Westminster Abbey, Buckingham Palace, the Tower of London, the Houses of Parliament and many other places. There are some big cut-away illustrations showing what goes on inside some of the best-known landmarks.

There are lots of surprising stories and historical details about them, too. For instance, you can find out about the three cathedrals that have been on the site of today's Saint Paul's, and about the man who stole the Crown Jewels from the Tower of London.

Regent's Park

As well as historic buildings London has more open spaces than almost any other city. This book has maps, stories and information about its world-famous parks, and tips on things you can see and do in them.

Household Cavalry

Near the end of the book you can find out about London life – its many annual festivals and events, its well-known spectacles, such as the Changing of the Guard, and surprising events like "beating the bounds" around the Tower of London.

There are tips on what and who to look out for around London's streets, interesting places to shop and some of the art galleries and theatres that put on events especially for young people.

At the back of the book there is a guide for London visitors – with addresses and opening times for all the places mentioned in this book, plus dates and places for special events. There is a telephone number with each entry, so you can call to check details before making a journey.

There are extra tips on activities run for young people and on further places to visit, and even some cockney rhyming slang to learn. There is a map of London on pages 56-57 showing sites of interest around the capital.

London's beginnings

The earliest prehistoric settlers in the London area lived along parts of the Thames Valley. Some of their flint tools have been found in river gravel. At this time it was mostly wild forested countryside.

In later prehistoric times the settlers became more organized. They lived in villages of huts made of timber, branches and clay (called wattle and daub). They hunted, fished and farmed.

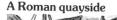
Early prehistoric settlers

A village in later prehistoric times

Early Roman Londinium

Roman London Bridge

Roman soldiers arrived to conquer Britain in AD43, and founded Londinium, now called London. They built a bridge over the Thames, and there has been a "London Bridge" in the same area ever since*.

A Roman quayside

Roman Londinium grew up on the northern side of the bridge. Products such as olive oil and wine were brought by ships from different parts of the Roman Empire and unloaded onto wooden quays along the river.

Boudicca in her chariot

In AD61 the native Iceni tribe, led by Queen Boudicca, rose up against the Romans. They burned Londinium to the ground and killed all its inhabitants. You can see a statue of Boudicca by Westminster Bridge.

The town rebuilt

Tiled roofs
Market stalls

Roman armies eventually defeated Boudicca. Londinium was rebuilt and was gradually surrounded with a wall of stone and brick which lasted for many centuries.

Inside the Roman wall low houses were built with bright red tiled roofs. There were probably temples, bath houses, shops and market stalls like the ones above.

You can still walk along part of the route of the old wall. The area once inside it is now the business district of modern London, called the City (see page 18).

The Basilica and Forum

The picture on the right is a reconstruction of the most important part of Roman Londinium, the Basilica and Forum. The Basilica was a business centre, and the Forum was a market place. Excavations have revealed the old Roman foundations. Gracechurch Street, in the City, now runs through the middle of this area.

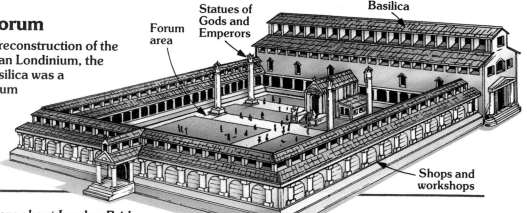
Forum area
Statues of Gods and Emperors
Basilica
Shops and workshops

4   *You can find out more about London Bridge on page 24.

Anglo-Saxon London

At the end of the fourth century AD the Roman Empire began to crumble and the Roman armies were recalled from Britain to defend Rome itself. Once they had left, tribes of people called Angles, Saxons and Jutes invaded and settled in Britain from Holland, Germany and Denmark. Together they are known as the Anglo-Saxons, and they established a new way of life in England.

In the town

Londinium in ruins

The Anglo-Saxons were farming people, who preferred to live outside towns. For a while London probably lay in ruins, but it eventually developed again, partly because its position on the river was good for trading.

Monks in the first Saint Paul's

Christianity gradually grew stronger in Anglo-Saxon Britain. In AD604 a cathedral was founded in London and named after the apostle, Saint Paul. There is still a cathedral on the site (see page 20).

In the ninth and tenth centuries the town suffered many attacks and occupations by heathen Danish Vikings. They sailed up the Thames in boats like the ones above, attacking and looting the town and setting up base there.

London Bridge is falling down

In 1014 Anglo-Saxons joined forces with Norwegian Vikings and sailed up the Thames to defeat Danish Vikings who were occupying London. A Norse poet of the time wrote about the battle and the story gave rise to the song "London Bridge is falling down".

The Danish warriors stood on London Bridge hurling spears down at the Norwegian Vikings, who retreated and pulled down roofs from nearby cottages to protect their boats. Then they attached ropes underneath the bridge and pulled it down.

Viking attacks on London only ended when Canute became King of England in 1016. He was a fierce Danish warrior who was converted to Christianity. He united the Danish invaders and the native Anglo-Saxons. Peace came and London prospered.

Edward's Abbey

A workman puts the final touch to the building. God blesses the Abbey. Edward's funeral procession

Seven years after Canute's death Edward the Confessor became King. He built the first great London building, Westminster Abbey, on the site of an old church called Saint Peter's. The Abbey was consecrated (blessed) at Christmas in 1065 and Edward died a week later. Since then it has been rebuilt. You can find out more about it on page 14.

The picture above shows the earliest illustration of the Abbey, from part of the Bayeux tapestry. It depicts the completion of the building, the consecration and Edward's burial there. During his lifetime he lived in a palace nearby which may have been Canute's old home. The Palace of Westminster (Houses of Parliament) now stands on the site (see page 16).

Medieval London

In 1066, after Edward the Confessor's death, William the Conqueror invaded England from France. The centuries from William's reign up to 1485 are known as the medieval period in English history.

The medieval City

The old Roman walls of the City of London were repaired and added to in medieval times. The picture on the right shows how a street within them might have looked.

There were many churches and some important monasteries in the medieval City. Some of the churches still exist, but the monasteries have disappeared. Only their names remain in places such as Whitefriars and Blackfriars.

Medieval shopping

Medieval Londoners could buy all kinds of things from street sellers, including food such as hot pies, fruit and strongly spiced meat. The sellers shouted out to advertise their wares, like some London stallholders do today.

Houses were built of timber frames filled with plaster.

Upper floors overhung those below.

Rubbish was thrown from windows into the street below.

Streets were often cobbled.

Street markets sold particular types of goods. For instance, there was a livestock market at Smithfield, where meat is still sold today. Animals were driven through the town on their way to market.

In the City many streets are named after medieval trades and shops. For instance, there is Threadneedle Street (where tailors once worked), Bread Street (a bakery area) and Milk Street (where cows were once kept for milking).

William's tower

The White Tower when first built

To keep an eye on his new subjects in the City of London William the Conqueror built the White Tower (part of today's Tower of London site). It is one of the few medieval buildings still remaining in London.

It was finished during the reign of his son, William Rufus. It got its name because it was built of pale stone. You can find out more about it on page 22.

Merchants and craftsmen

Banners hung in the Guildhall

Merchants and craftsmen gathered together inside the City walls to live and work in particular areas.

They formed powerful associations called Guilds (see page 18), and had their own halls and coats of arms. Some of their banners are shown above. One of the London merchants was elected Mayor of the City every year, and this is still carried on.

Entertainment

Target   Tilting pole

On medieval holidays Londoners liked entertainments such as jousting, wrestling, bear-baiting, archery and hunting in the fields and woods outside the City walls.

There were often carnival-style processions, when the streets were decked with flags and tapestries. Sometimes sports were played in boats on the Thames, like the water-borne tilting game shown above.

Tudor and Elizabethan London

Henry the Seventh came to the throne in 1485. He began the Tudor line of monarchs (Tudor was his family name). He was succeeded by his son, Henry the Eighth, and grandchildren, Edward the Sixth, Mary the First and Elizabeth the First. The period of her reign is given the special name "Elizabethan" (1559-1603).

During the Tudors' time the London area grew and prospered as the centre of the country's Royal Court, government and trade. By 1600 about 200,000 people lived either within the old City walls or over London Bridge at Southwark.

A ruined monastery

Henry the Eighth separated the English from the Roman Catholic church, and abolished the monasteries. Many London monastery buildings were converted to houses, or pulled down for their building materials.

Henry the Eighth out hunting

The Tudors had many palaces in the London area. They also established Royal deer parks for hunting. You can find out more about Richmond deer park and the Tudor palace at Hampton Court Palace on page 42.

Countryside around the City

Much of today's London was still meadows and fields in Tudor times. Cows grazed where Oxford Street now stands, and it only took fifteen minutes to walk from the Thames through the City to the countryside beyond.

On the river

Elizabethan galleons

The Tudors built up the nation's navy, constructing new dockyards for magnificent galleons like the ones shown above. Some of these ships left London to explore new parts of the world, such as America and India. The best way to travel around the London areas itself was by ferry-boat up and down the Thames.

John Stow

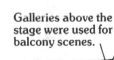

Life in Elizabethan London was recorded by John Stow, a retired tailor who wrote a survey of the City. He visited buildings, questioned residents and studied old records. Stow is buried in the church of Saint Andrew Undershaft, in the City. Every year a memorial service is held there (see page 52).

Tudor playhouses

Elizabethan London saw the construction of the first theatres, called playhouses. The most famous of these was the Globe in Southwark, south of the Thames. The picture on the right shows the second Globe; the first building was burned down in 1613.

Shakespeare owned a share of the theatre and wrote his plays for performance there. Acting was not thought to be respectable in those days. Women were not allowed to act at all, and men took their parts. Theatre audiences were far noisier and rowdier than they are today.

Galleries above the stage were used for balcony scenes.

The theatre had no roof. If it rained plays were called off.

Wooden galleries for the audience and musicians

It was cheapest to stand in front of the stage and watch.

7

Seventeenth century London

Elizabeth the First, the last of the Tudors, died in 1603. She was succeeded by James the First, who was already King James the Sixth of Scotland. He united the two countries.

James was followed by his son, Charles the First, and his grandson Charles the Second. They are called the Stuart kings (their family name). During the time of the Stuarts there was much political upheaval in the country, and important changes in the layout of London.

Civil war

The beheading of Charles the First

In the 1640s England was torn by civil war between the Royalist forces of Charles the First and the Parliamentarian forces of Cromwell, who used London as their headquarters. In 1649 Charles the First was beheaded in London, but in 1660 the monarchy returned and Charles the Second was crowned in Westminster Abbey.

Samuel Pepys

Pepys writing his diary.

Historians have learned a lot about life in Charles the Second's London by reading the diaries of Samuel Pepys, who was born and lived in the capital. He held a high position as Secretary to the Admiralty, and often went to the King's Court. He wrote his diary in six notebooks, recording his daily life.

The Plague

People fleeing London

Plague houses

A plague pit

Filthy conditions in seventeenth century London helped to spread epidemics like the plague. In 1665 the plague probably killed about 100,000 people, one in three of those who stayed in London. Many people fled to the countryside with their belongings.

The disease was carried by black rats from ships in the port. It was transferred to humans by fleas. People who caught the plague were locked up in their houses with their families, and their doors were marked with a red warning cross.

There was no cure for the plague. The first signs were black and purple blotches and sores; then the disease developed quickly and could kill in a few days. Bodies were collected from the streets, taken away in carts and buried in large plague pits.

The Great Fire of London

In 1666 a huge fire swept away many of the old medieval wooden buildings in the City. It began in the kitchen of the King's baker in Pudding Lane, and lasted for five days, destroying four-fifths of the City including Saint Paul's Cathedral.

After the fire a monument was erected near where it started (see page 19), and the old houses were rebuilt in terraces of brick along the lines of the old medieval streets. The architect Sir Christopher Wren set about rebuilding Saint Paul's. You can find out more about it on page 20.

Eighteenth century London

In 1714 George the First came to the throne. He was a member of the German branch of the Royal family, the Hanovers, and his family dynasty reigned until 1837. In the eighteenth century Britain was one of the world's most powerful nations, with London as the centre of its trade.

River business

Ships brought in goods from all over the world, unloading them onto "legal quays", like the one shown on the right. Here they were checked by Customs men and a tax was levied on cargo. A lot of smuggling probably went on, when goods were secretly unloaded without being checked.

Customs men checking cargo

London life

A criminal in the stocks

The ill-lit streets of London were full of beggars, pickpockets and thieves. Convicted criminals were put in the stocks, to be pelted with rubbish and stones. Sometimes they were hanged at Tyburn, near today's Marble Arch.

Financial dealers in Exchange Alley

Financial business began to develop in London in the eighteenth century. Many of the deals were done in coffee houses, especially in a street called Exchange Alley, site of today's Stock Exchange (see page 19).

In a pleasure garden

Pleasure gardens became popular in eighteenth century London. They were like early amusement parks, with stalls and entertainers. You can find out more about London parks on page 32.

The British Museum

Early Museum displays

The British Museum opened in 1759 and was made up of the collection of historical objects acquired by Sir Hans Sloane, a royal physician and antique collector, who died in 1753. The picture above shows how the museum might have looked at that time. The exhibits were not put in any order, so it must have looked like a junk shop. Since then the collection has grown enormously. You can find out more about it on page 36.

William Hogarth

Hogarth in his London studio

Writers, artists and actors made eighteenth century London a lively centre of art and literature. This picture shows a famous London artist, William Hogarth. Many of his paintings tell a story to show up hypocrisy, greed and corruption in London. London scenes were also painted by other eighteenth century artists such as Canaletto. You can see some of this work in London's art galleries (see page 54).

Nineteenth century London

In 1837 Queen Victoria came to the throne, aged 18. By the time of her death in 1901 London was a very different city. It had grown enormously due to industrial progress, population growth and the network of railways which had brought many parts of England within easy reach of the capital. In the Victorian era London was the centre of world trade and a powerful British empire. Better street lighting, sanitation, roads and transport gradually developed.

Docks and steamers

A Thames steamer

In the nineteenth century ships delivered goods to London from all over the Empire. Large docks were built to provide a safe place for them to anchor.

Shipbuilding was changed completely by the invention of the steam engine and iron ships. By 1860 London had the largest number of shipyards in the world.

The picture above shows a busy Thames scene in mid-century. It was crowded with boats, including "penny steamers" which made regular trips along the river.

Transport and building

Open trucks pulled by a steam engine

‡Cannon Street station

Parliament being rebuilt

The coming of the railways changed London for ever. It meant that people could now commute to work from elsewhere. The first London underground railway is shown above. It opened in 1863 between Paddington and the City.

Grand railway stations, such as Paddington, Euston and Cannon Street, were built at the centre of a network of railway lines going to different parts of Britain. They looked impressive to encourage people to travel by train.

Much of present day London was built in Victorian times. Some buildings were very grand, such as the Houses of Parliament, rebuilt after a fire in 1834 (see page 16). Others were built for workers, in terraced rows.

Victorian slums

In Victorian London the poor were crowded into rotting houses, where they often starved or died of disease. Some of the worst-off were poor children. They were sent out from the age of four or five to make a few pennies by doing things like begging, pickpocketing and chimney sweeping.

Campaigners, such as the author Charles Dickens, shocked the public by writing about these things, and in 1870 a new law was passed which meant that all children between the ages of 5 and 12 had to go to school.

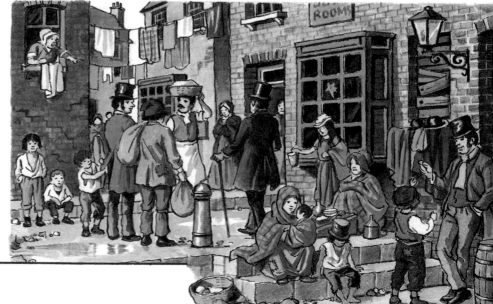

Twentieth century London

London has spread outwards more and more in the twentieth century. Many people now live in suburbs far away from their work and travel to the centre by train, bus and car. The population is now over seven million, and it is by far the biggest city in Britain.

Early 1900s

The Ritz Hotel, opened in 1905.

London was an elegant centre of entertainment in Edwardian times (during the reign of Edward the Seventh, 1901-1910). New luxury hotels, restaurants and theatres were built, especially in the West End area.

London's first escalator, installed in Harrods in 1908.

In the early 1900s big department stores were built in the West End, for instance Selfridges and Harrods. They were the first to house lots of different goods in one building. You can find out more about London shopping on page 48.

An early London bus

Today's London transport system began to develop around this time. In 1890 the first electric underground train ran from the City to Stockwell, and in 1905 motor buses appeared. You can find out more about transport on page 46.

War destruction

Bomb damage in a London suburb

London was heavily bombed during the Second World War, and some of its most historic buildings were destroyed or badly damaged. One of the worst hit areas was the oldest part, the City, around Saint Paul's. The cathedral itself was not badly damaged.

← The NatWest Tower, 198m high.

Modern buildings have since appeared on the old bombsites. For instance, the City area, once the heart of medieval London, has been completely changed by modern high-rise blocks, including the tallest building in Britain, the NatWest Tower.

The Museum of London

One of London's newest building complexes is the Barbican Centre, to the north of the City. It includes high-rise blocks of flats, a theatre and concert hall, art gallery and restaurants. Nearby is the Museum of London. Its displays tell the story of London from prehistory onwards. These include reconstructions of Roman life, Viking weapons, a scene with sound effects depicting the Fire of London, and the Lord Mayor's coach. Some of its displays are labelled in the plan on the right.

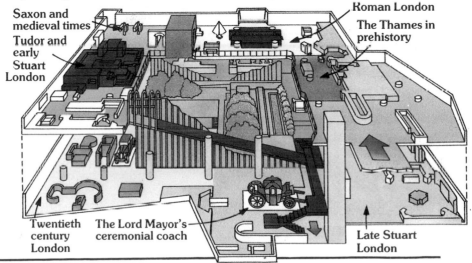

Saxon and medieval times
Tudor and early Stuart London
Roman London
The Thames in prehistory
Twentieth century London
The Lord Mayor's ceremonial coach
Late Stuart London

11

The growth of London

London has grown over the centuries into a huge sprawling city, especially so since the railways were built. They linked the capital to surrounding villages, which lost their separate identities and became residential suburbs. Many of them are now incorporated in the area known as Greater London. The map below shows how the capital has spread since medieval times.

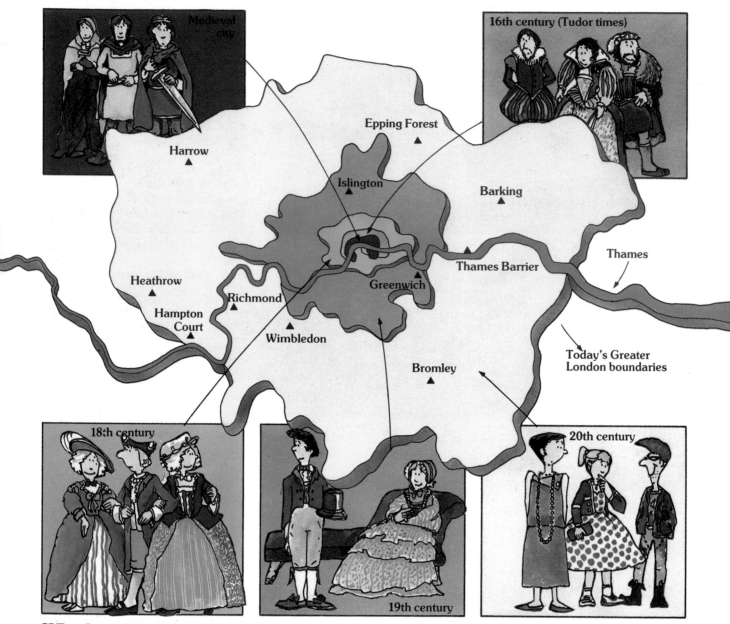

Medieval city

16th century (Tudor times)

Epping Forest

Harrow

Islington

Barking

Heathrow

Thames

Richmond

Greenwich

Thames Barrier

Hampton Court

Wimbledon

Today's Greater London boundaries

Bromley

18th century

19th century

20th century

Why London grew

⭐ London's importance and prosperity over the centuries is largely due to the River Thames. The river provided a good communications and trading route, and enabled ships to reach the port from all over the world.

⭐ London has been the centre of Britain's transport network since Roman times, with roads radiating outwards to all parts of the country. This has helped industry to grow, and many people have come to London for work.

⭐ For centuries London has been the home of government and of the monarch. This has ensured its position as Britain's capital. Its importance has meant that it has always been a centre of trends and fashions, too.

East and west

Parts of London have developed in different ways. The contrast is great between two famous areas, the West End and the East End. In medieval times rich and noble families lived only in the City. But gradually they moved west, to the area which became known as the "West End". It still has many expensive houses and shops.

People came to the East End to find work on ships and in the docks. At the end of the nineteenth century the docks began to decline, leading to unemployment and terrible poverty around them. Now the East End has become an area of small industries and housing, with many high-rise tower block developments replacing the old slums.

Settlers through the ages

People of many nationalities have settled in London. They have come to find work or because of religious persecution in their own countries. Often they have set up their own communities in one particular area.

In Anglo-Saxon times Danish Viking invaders settled in London. They lived in an area outside the City walls, where they built a church, Saint Clement Dane. There is still a church on the same site (see page 18).

Petty France

In the seventeenth century Protestant Huguenots moved from France to London to escape religious persecution. In Westminster, where some settled, there is still a street called Petty France, (meaning "little France").

Jews were first encouraged to settle in the City of London by William the Conqueror. They lived in a street called Old Jewry, which still exists today. Since the late 1800s many more Jews have settled in London, especially in the East End. They fled from persecution in Eastern Europe and Germany. ▼

Old Jewry

Since the Second World War people have come to live and work in London from the Commonwealth countries of India and Pakistan. They have set up many businesses, and celebrate their own religious festivals.

Many people have come from Arab countries, too, and have set up temples for their Islamic faith.

The Islamic temple in Regent's Park ▼

Gerrard street in Soho's Chinatown

Chinese people have come to live in Chinatown, an area in Soho, where the streets are lined with Chinese restaurants and food shops. In January or February the Chinese New Year is celebrated here with a colourful parade (see page 53).

Notting Hill Carnival

Many people have come from the Commonwealth countries of the West Indies to settle in London. In August the West Indian community holds a Caribbean-style carnival around the Portobello Road area of Notting Hill, with lots of decorated floats, dancing in the streets, reggae groups and steel bands.

Westminster Abbey

Westminster Abbey is one of the oldest buildings in London and one of the most important religious centres in the country. Many kings, queens and famous people are buried or commemorated there. Its founder, Edward the Confessor, was made a saint after his death (see page 5) and is buried in a special chapel dedicated to him.

The Abbey legend

Saint Peter and the ferryman

The first church on the Abbey site was Saint Peter's, probably built in the seventh century. The area was then a marshy place called Thorney Island. A legend says that Saint Peter was ferried over to bless the church. He told the ferryman to cast his nets, which quickly filled with salmon.

Monastic life

The old Abbey garden

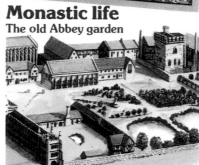

For hundreds of years the Abbey was the home of Benedictine monks. They cultivated farmland around the Abbey. You can still see their cloisters and visit the 900-year-old Abbey garden, where the monks grew medicinal herbs. Concerts are now held there in summer.

The new Abbey

Henry supervising architects

Two hundred years after the death of Edward the Confessor, Henry the Third had the old Abbey demolished, and began rebuilding it in a new style around a magnificent new shrine to honour Edward. Henry had to pawn his own jewels to raise funds for the expensive building.

Rebuilding

The picture above shows workmen busy rebuilding the Abbey. They began work under a master mason called Henry de Reyns, who was responsible for the design and construction of the building. Work continued for centuries, with many other architects and sculptors.

The picture below shows the groundplan of Westminster Abbey, labelled with points of interest. You can look around the building in between the church services held there daily.

The coronation of the Queen

The Abbey has been the scene of every royal coronation since William the Conqueror in 1066. Queen Elizabeth the Second was crowned in front of the High Altar in 1953, by the Archbishop of Canterbury. A congregation of 8,000 people attended the Abbey that day.

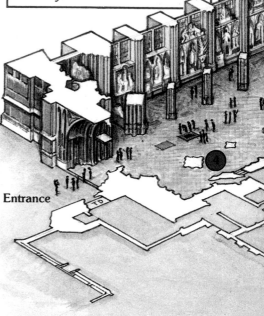

Entrance

4 Near the entrance to the Abbey you can see the tomb of the Unknown Warrior. It commemorates all the ordinary British soldiers who died in the First World War.

The body of an unknown First World War British soldier is buried here, brought from a French battlefield.

2 Nine English kings and queens are buried in Saint Edward's Chapel around the Shrine, including Henry the Fifth. When he was buried his battle horses were led up to the High Altar.

Edward's tomb

Monarchs are crowned while sitting on the Coronation throne, kept in the Chapel. The Stone of Scone, a symbol of Scottish Royalty, is kept underneath it.

Stone of Scone

3 Henry the Seventh built the magnificent chapel at the eastern end of the Abbey. There are many English kings and queens buried there. One of the tombs contains bones found hidden in the Tower of London, probably those of the princes murdered there (see page 23).

Battle of Britain Memorial Window

Tombs of Mary and Elizabeth the First

Admission fee beyond this point

High altar

Choir

Chapter House

The Chapel of the Pyx

Nave

Cloisters

The Deanery

5 Part of the Abbey is a brass-rubbing centre. Brasses are pictures put on tombs, and the centre has many replicas. Using the materials provided you can rub over them to make a copy.

6 Parts of the Abbey are set aside for the memorials and tombs of different types of people, such as statesmen, scientists and musicians. In Poets'Corner many famous British poets, playwrights and novelists are buried or commemorated.

Memorial to Shakespeare in Poets' Corner

7 In the Museum of Abbey Treasures you can see models of the Crown Jewels, used for coronation rehearsals. There are also effigies on display, lifelike models of famous people made after their death. These include Elizabeth of York. A copy of her face was traditionally used for the pictures of queens on playing cards.

The Houses of Parliament

The Houses of Parliament are the seat of British Government*. Members of Parliament (MPs) are elected to sit in its Commons Chamber, where they propose and pass new laws. In the Lords Chamber Peers (people with noble titles) discuss and amend these laws.

In Victoria Tower millions of parliamentary documents are kept, including copies of every law passed by Parliament since the 1400s. A Union flag flies on the tower when Parliament is sitting during daylight hours.

Old Palace Yard

Royal Entrance

Westminster Hall

Westminster Hall

Westminster Hall is one of the ▲ few remaining parts of a medieval royal palace once built on today's site. It has an impressive hammerbeam roof decorated with massive carved angels. It has been used for royal Christmas feasts, coronation banquets, and State trials.

The great fire

The old palace ablaze

In 1834 most of the old palace ▲ buildings were destroyed by fire, caused by an oven which caught alight. Sir Charles Barry rebuilt the palace with over 1,000 rooms, in a medieval style called Gothic. The intricate stonework decoration was done by his partner, Augustus Pugin.

Famous events

◄ At midnight on November 4, 1605, Guy Fawkes was discovered in a cellar beneath the House of Lords, about to set light to a pile of gunpowder barrels. Every autumn his capture is still celebrated.

In 1642 Charles the First went to ► the House of Commons to arrest five MPs, who criticized his rule. They foiled him by escaping. Since then, the Sovereign has never been allowed into the Commons.

Charles in the House

The monarch's throne

◄ Parliament is reopened in November after a summer break with a ceremony called the State Opening, when the monarch makes a speech from a throne in the Lords Chamber. An official called "Black Rod" is sent to the Commons to summon MPs to hear the speech.

The Houses of Parliament has over 1,000 rooms, and 3km (2 miles) of corridors – the distance from Saint Paul's Cathedral to Parliament.

*You need to make special arrangements to see around the building (see page 58).

2 In the Robing Room the monarch puts on the Robes of State and the Imperial State Crown before opening Parliament. The room has its own throne, and decorations based on ancient tales. The walls are painted with scenes from the story of King Arthur.

The throne in the Robing Room.

3 The Central Lobby is the main reception area, decorated with intricate mosaics. On his way to debates the House of Commons Speaker walks in procession through here with the Mace, the symbol of royal authority.

The Mace

4 Big Ben is the huge bell in the clock of Saint Stephen's Tower. It may have been named after Sir Benjamin Hall, who supervised the rebuilding of Parliament, or after a famous Victorian prize fighter. When Parliament is sitting at night a light shines above the clock.

Westminster Hall

7 The House of Commons is decorated in a simple style with tiers of green seats. The Government sits on one side of the room with the Opposition on the other.

There are stripes on the floor in front of each side. The distance between the stripes is the distance between two drawn swords.

The House of Commons

5 The Royal Gallery leads from the Robing Room to the Lords Chamber. On each side of the long hall there are huge paintings by the Victorian artist Daniel Maclisse. They show the battles of Trafalgar and Waterloo.

6 The Lord Chancellor is in charge of the House of Lords. He sits on the Woolsack. It is a cushion stuffed with wool to symbolize what was once England's chief source of wealth.

The Woolsack

8 The MPs' Tea Terrace stretches along the riverside, and you can see it from Westminster Bridge.

9 The Speaker's rooms are the living quarters of the House of Commons Speaker, who keeps order during debates.

The City of London

The City of London occupies one square mile in the middle of the capital. It once made up the entire town of London, surrounded by the wall first built by the Romans (see page 4). It is now Britain's banking and financial centre, but there are still many reminders of its historical past.

The Mayor

The Lord Mayor's procession

Special guard

The Mayor's coach

The City area has always been governed separately from the rest of the capital. It has its own Lord Mayor who serves a one year term of office and lives in the Mansion House during that time.

Every November the Lord Mayor's Show is held. The new Mayor travels in a magnificent red and gold coach* through the City to the Law Courts in the Strand, to be sworn in.

On the journey he is guarded by the Honourable Artillery Company of Pikemen and Musketeers, who wear Cromwellian Civil War uniforms. Many carnival floats follow.

Guilds and the Guildhall

Mayors are chosen from members of the Livery Companies, City Guilds which have been granted the special right to a uniform. The Guilds were groups set up by medieval craftsmen to look after their trades. They once controlled all City business, but now they work mainly for charity.

The Guildhall is the civic centre of the City. You can visit its clock museum and medieval hall, where Livery Company banners are hung. In the hall there are two huge models of Gog and Magog, legendary ancient British giants. The statues are based on models paraded at medieval midsummer festivals.

Magog

Gog

The front of the Guildhall

City churches

There are 39 churches in the City, 11 dating from before the Great Fire, and 23 designed by Sir Christopher Wren to replace those burned down. Many of them feature in the old nursery rhyme which begins "Oranges and Lemons, say the bells of Saint Clement's".

Saint Mary-le-Bow is famous for its "Bow Bells", which used to ring daily. A true Londoner, a Cockney, has to be born within the sound of the bells.

Saint Mary-le-Bow

In the eighteenth century a baker made a wedding cake replica of of the steeple of Saint Bride's, built by Wren. It soon became the fashion, and is the origin of the tiered wedding cakes made today.

Saint Bride's

The church of Saint Clement Dane is just outside the City. It is probably the church mentioned in first verse of the nursery rhyme "Oranges and Lemons".

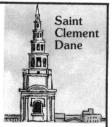

Saint Clement Dane

The Temple Church was built by a group of medieval knights called the Knights Templars. Inside there are knights' effigies, and a tiny cell where knights who broke the rules of the Order were imprisoned.

Temple Church

City business

World banks and trading companies have offices in the City. The biggest is the Bank of England, which looks after the accounts of the British government. It has its own nickname, "the old lady of Threadneedle Street".

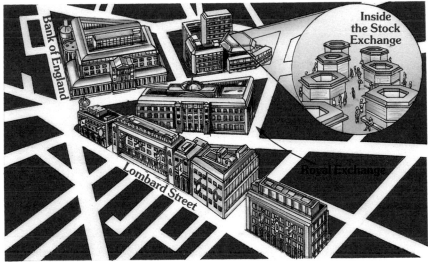

The Stock Exchange is where company shares are bought and sold, although no money actually changes hands. Originally everything was done by word of mouth, and settled up later. This led to much confusion and today the whole Stock Exchange is computerized.

Lombard Street in the City was named after medieval Italian gold and silver merchants called Lombards. They were the first to establish a banking system in the country. There are still lots of banks in the street and many have medieval-type decorated signs hanging outside.

City ceremonies

There are many annual ceremonies in the City, most dating back to medieval times. Some are listed below.

Quit Rents: The City pays a ▶ yearly rent to the monarch for two ancient properties granted to them. The rent is six horseshoes, 61 nails, a billhook and a hatchet.

◀ **Boar's head gift**: The Butchers' Company presents the Mayor with a boar's head on a silver platter every year, as a payment for lands granted in the fourteenth century.

The Knollys rose: In June the ▶ Lord Mayor is presented with a rose by the Company of Watermen and Lightermen. It was a fine imposed on Lady Knollys in the 1400s, for building without permission.

The Monument

The Monument, shown below, was built to commemorate the Fire of London. You can climb to the top for a good view of the City.

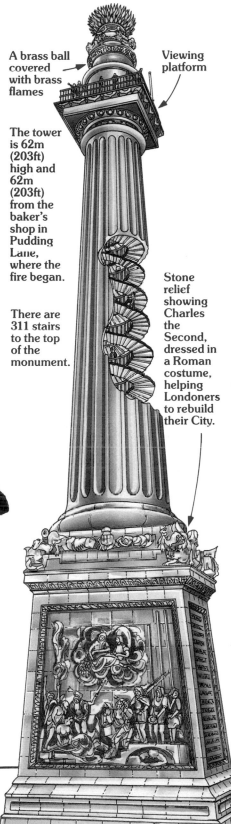

A brass ball covered with brass flames

Viewing platform

The tower is 62m (203ft) high and 62m (203ft) from the baker's shop in Pudding Lane, where the fire began.

There are 311 stairs to the top of the monument.

Stone relief showing Charles the Second, dressed in a Roman costume, helping Londoners to rebuild their City.

Saint Paul's Cathedral

Saint Paul's is the cathedral of the City of London. Up to 3 million people visit it each year, and its 111m (364ft) high dome has become a symbol of London throughout the world. The cut-away picture on the right shows some of its most interesting features.

Old Saint Paul's

Old Saint Paul's in ruins

A medieval cathedral of Saint Paul's was built on the site of an Anglo-Saxon church (see page 5). After Tudor times the building was neglected. People drove cattle to market through the Nave, which they nicknamed "Paul's Walk", shown above.

The old cathedral was completely destroyed by the Great Fire of London in 1666. People put their belongings in the church, thinking it was safe, but the fire soon reached it. It was so hot it turned the church bells into molten metal.

Rebuilding

Sir Christopher Wren

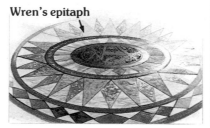

Wren's epitaph

The architect Sir Christopher Wren was commissioned to rebuild Saint Paul's. He made several plans before one was accepted. In the Crypt of the church you can see scale models of his rejected designs.

Wren is buried in the cathedral Crypt. The last line of his epitaph is also set into the floor underneath the centre of the cathedral dome. Translated from Latin it reads: "If you seek his monument, look around you."

Wartime Saint Paul's

During the Second World War the City was very badly bombed in the Blitz, and two bombs fell on Saint Paul's. During the bombing the church was guarded by volunteers who were members of "Saint Paul's Watch". You can see their monument on the floor of the Nave.

Saint Paul's during a night-time bombing raid

1 The Crypt extends under the whole building. Here you can see many memorials to famous people, including the tomb of Lord Nelson. There is a display of Cathedral treasures, including priest's robes

A robe embroidered with City churches

2 Big Paul, the heaviest bell in the country, is in the northern bell tower at the front of Saint Paul's. It rings every weekday at 1pm to let people know that it is lunchtime.

Another bell, Big Tom, tolls when a monarch or important churchmen die. The church bells in the other tower are rung on Sundays and to celebrate great occasions.

3 In the north side of the Nave there is a huge monument to the Duke of Wellington. On the top the figure of the Duke sits on his favourite horse, named Copenhagen.

Front entrance

4 The dome of Saint Paul's is actually made of two domes, one inside the other. Running around the inside is a balcony called the Whispering Gallery. It gets its name because a whisper directed along the wall on one side of the dome can be very clearly heard on the other side.

6 The American Memorial Chapel is at the eastern end of the church. It commemorates the Americans who died in the Second World War. Their names are written in a roll of honour kept in a glass and gold case. Around the screens of the chapel there are carvings of American animals and birds.

5 The saucer domes in the Choir are decorated with Victorian mosaics made up of thousands of tiny pieces of glass. They depict living things created by God: land animals, water creatures and birds. There are other mosaics around the building.

Whispering Gallery

Outer dome

Brick cone

Inner dome with scenes from the life of Saint Paul

Choir

Nave

South Transept

7 The effigy of John Donne was the only Saint Paul's statue to survive the Great Fire. Donne was a seventeenth century poet, who became Dean of the Cathedral in 1621. His statue shows him dressed from head to toe in a shroud. He dressed and modelled for the memorial before he died.

8 The Choir has wooden stalls carved for Wren by Grinling Gibbons. A Master Carver works full-time restoring the carvings in the church. You can spot his work because it is a different shade to the original wood. Eventually the new wood will darken and blend in.

21

The Tower of London

The Tower of London was begun by William the Conqueror in 1078 as a castle and palace. Since then it has been expanded, and used as an armoury, a zoo, a royal mint and a notorious prison.

Tower prisoners

Elizabeth   Raleigh   Anne Boleyn

Many people have been locked in the Tower, for religious beliefs or suspected treason. Famous prisoners have included Anne Boleyn, Sir Walter Raleigh and Elizabeth the First (when a Princess). Spies were imprisoned here during both World Wars.

Stretching on a torture rack

Some prisoners could walk in the grounds, live in comfortable rooms and receive visitors. Others were locked in tiny freezing cells, and tortured for confessions. You can see old torture instruments on display.

There have been several successful escapes from the Tower. Ranulf Flambard, the first known prisoner, was also the first to escape, in 1101. He climbed down the walls using a rope which had been smuggled to him inside a wine barrel.

Beheading block and axe

Many convicted prisoners were publicly executed on Tower Hill. Some were beheaded privately on Tower Green. In the Tower Armoury there is a block and axe used for a beheading in 1747.

The Crown Jewels

Imperial State Crown

Orb

Star of Africa

The Crown Jewels are kept in the Jewel House at the Tower. The collection includes Saint Edward's Crown, used for the coronation ceremony, and the Imperial State Crown, containing 3,000 precious jewels. The royal sceptre contains the biggest cut diamond in the world, the "Star of Africa".

In 1671 a daring attempt was made to steal the Crown Jewels, by a man named Captain Blood. His gang attacked a guard and ran off with the treasure, but were caught trying to escape. Captain Blood was later pardoned by Charles the Second. Some think the King organized the raid to raise money.

The Tower of London site, shown below, has developed to its present size over hundreds of years. There are many interesting rooms and displays to see.

A group of ravens live at the Tower. The tradition goes that if they disappear the building will collapse. For centuries a royal zoo was kept in the grounds. It once included a polar bear, who fished and swam in the moat, now drained.

Outer walls

Chapel where famous prisoners are buried.

Devereux Tower

Beauchamp Tower

The Beefeaters (Yeoman Warders) guard the Tower. They used to be the monarch's private bodyguard. "Beefeater" was a medieval nickname for well-fed servants. They wear a Tudor-style uniform of blue or red.

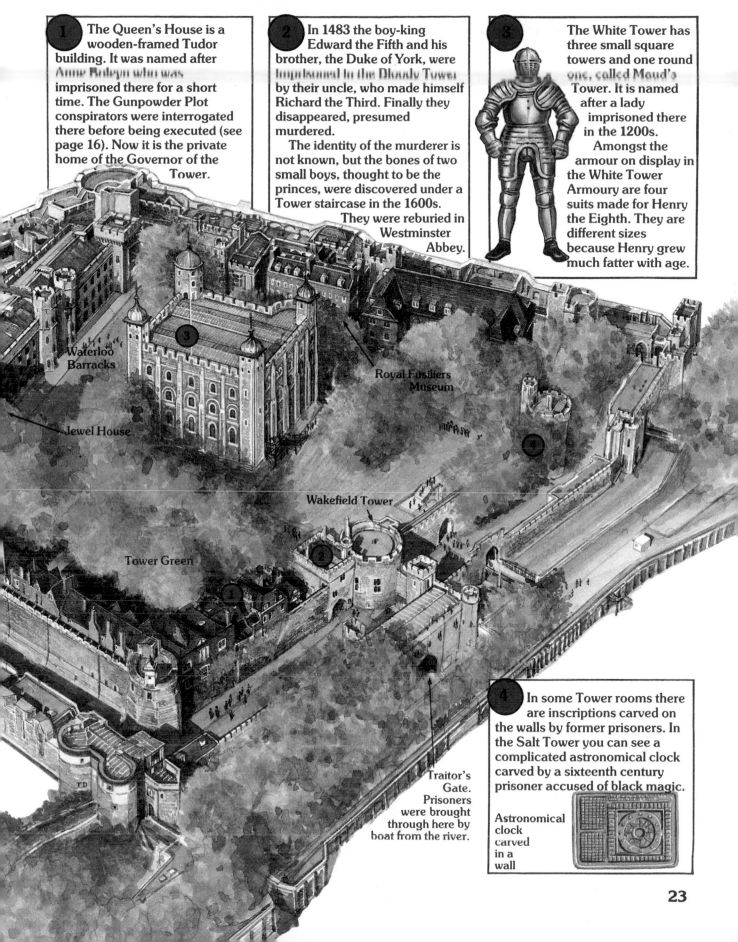

1 The Queen's House is a wooden-framed Tudor building. It was named after Anne Boleyn who was imprisoned there for a short time. The Gunpowder Plot conspirators were interrogated there before being executed (see page 16). Now it is the private home of the Governor of the Tower.

2 In 1483 the boy-king Edward the Fifth and his brother, the Duke of York, were imprisoned in the Bloody Tower by their uncle, who made himself Richard the Third. Finally they disappeared, presumed murdered.

The identity of the murderer is not known, but the bones of two small boys, thought to be the princes, were discovered under a Tower staircase in the 1600s. They were reburied in Westminster Abbey.

3 The White Tower has three small square towers and one round one, called Maud's Tower. It is named after a lady imprisoned there in the 1200s.

Amongst the armour on display in the White Tower Armoury are four suits made for Henry the Eighth. They are different sizes because Henry grew much fatter with age.

Waterloo Barracks

Jewel House

Royal Fusiliers Museum

Wakefield Tower

Tower Green

Traitor's Gate. Prisoners were brought through here by boat from the river.

4 In some Tower rooms there are inscriptions carved on the walls by former prisoners. In the Salt Tower you can see a complicated astronomical clock carved by a sixteenth century prisoner accused of black magic.

Astronomical clock carved in a wall

23

The River Thames

London developed as a centre of international trade because of its position on the River Thames. By the nineteenth century it was one of the busiest docklands in the world, handling Britain's huge import and export trade. The river is no longer important for business, and is now used mainly by pleasure boats.

London bridges

City side

Bridge gate

Old London Bridge as it once looked, based on a seventeenth century engraving by John Visscher

Southwark side

A wooden bridge, called London Bridge, existed from Roman times until the twelfth century, when it was rebuilt in stone with a street of houses along it. This structure lasted for more than 600 years.

The old stone bridge, shown above, became London's most famous landmark. Until 1750 it was the only bridge over the Thames in London. It gradually crumbled and was demolished.

A new bridge was built in 1831 to replace the old one. This in turn was demolished in 1967 and rebuilt in Lake Havasu City, USA, as a tourist attraction. The present London Bridge opened in 1973.

Bridge stories

Heads on the bridge gate.

Old London Bridge was built on stone arches resting on a series of piers. The houses along it often had shops at street level. At one end there was a stone gateway, where the heads of executed traitors were stuck on top of poles to rot away.

On the bridge

The road over the bridge was only about 4m (13ft) wide between the shops. It was so narrow it often jammed with people, horses and carts. In 1733 a "keep left" rule was enforced to keep the traffic moving. This became the rule of the road.

A Frost Fair

The bridge acted as a dam and slowed down the river, so that during winter it often froze upstream. Sometimes Frost Fairs were held, when stalls and entertainments were set up on the ice – puppet shows, football games and even barbecues.

River sights

There are many things to see and do along the Thames. Some are shown below.

Kathleen and May

Saint Katharine's Dock

To relieve overcrowding on the River in the 1800s big new docks were built. They were deep-water basins connected to the Thames by canals and locks. Now they have become office, housing and leisure areas.

Saint Katharine's Dock is now a marina, with shops and cafés around it. There is a lock connecting the dock to the Thames, and you can sometimes see it being used by pleasure boats going in and out.

In Saint Mary Overy Dock you can visit the Kathleen and May, which has recently been restored. She is one of the last remaining wooden sailing schooners, and once traded around the British coast, with four seamen on board.

HMS Belfast

Victoria Embankment

Cleopatra's Needle

HMS Belfast was built in 1938 and served in the Second World War. It is moored permanently on the Thames and is open as a Museum. You can visit different parts of the ship, including the engine room and the Captain's bridge.

In the 1800s three embankments were built along the Thames, with gas mains, sewage pipes and underground railways hidden inside them. There are pavements, benches and strings of lights laid out along them.

Cleopatra's Needle on Victoria Embankment is an ancient Egyptian monument, shipped to London in the 1870s. Victorian objects are buried underneath it, including newspapers, a railway timetable and a box of cigars.

Tower Bridge

Tower Bridge is the only Thames bridge which can be raised. The road over the bridge is built on two central sections called bascules, which open two or three times a week to let ships through. There are displays inside the bridge on its history.

A bus was once caught on the bridge as it began to open. It leapt across the opening bascules to safety.

Walkways, with good views of London

Exhibitions about the bridge

South bank

Museum with original lifting machinery

Bascules opening

Bridge mechanisms

Covent Garden

Open-air markets have existed in London since Roman times. Covent Garden is one of the most famous; for hundreds of years a fruit, flower and vegetable market was held here. Now it is a lively centre of entertainment, restaurants, shops and craft stalls.

Early times

Covent Garden was once a convent garden belonging to the monks of Westminster Abbey, hence its name. The monks grew vegetable produce for themselves, and what they didn't need they sold off, beginning the market tradition on the site. They also farmed a long field, called Long Acre, now a busy street running alongside Covent Garden.

The old Piazza

In the 1630s the architect Inigo Jones laid out London's first formal square in Covent Garden, called the Piazza. He built houses around it in a classical Italian style, fronted by arched walkways called colonnades. The originals no longer exist, although part of the square, Bedford Chambers, has been rebuilt in the old style.

Today's buildings

Saint Paul's

Old Central Market

Market rules on the wall

Inigo Jones' church, Saint Paul's, still overlooks today's Piazza. It has a grand porch (called a portico) facing the square and a quiet garden at the back. It is known as the actors' church, because it serves nearby theatres.

In 1830 the ramshackle sheds and stalls which made up the old market were replaced by the Central Market buildings in the middle of the Piazza. They were linked together by glass roofs, and housed fruit and vegetable traders.

The buildings have been restored and are now used as shops and cafes, although you can still see the old market rules written up on the walls. The old flower market building is now the London Transport Museum (see page 47).

The old market

The old fruit and vegetable market was a bustling lively place. It opened at about 4am when produce was delivered from country farms and sold from stalls to shopkeepers and restaurants. Goods were unloaded by porters, experts at carrying boxes and baskets on their heads. The market moved to Nine Elms in Vauxhall in 1971*.

*There is more about markets on page 49.

Covent Garden today

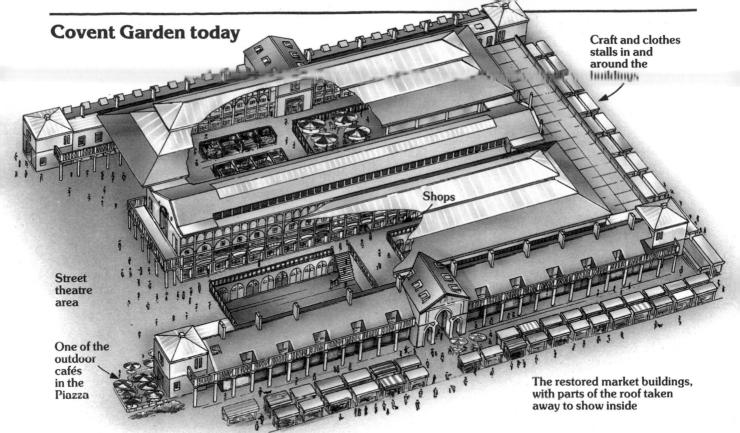

Craft and clothes stalls in and around the buildings

Shops

Street theatre area

One of the outdoor cafés in the Piazza

The restored market buildings, with parts of the roof taken away to show inside

In the restored market building there are lots of small shops, where you can buy everything from kitchen equipment and garden herbs to toys and clothes.

Theatres

There have always been many theatres around the Covent Garden area. One of the most famous is the Royal Opera House, home of the Royal Opera and Ballet companies. The most well-known opera singers in the world have performed there. You can sometimes hear echoes of the performances in the street below.

The Royal Opera House

There are also stalls selling original art and craft work, such as handmade pottery, jewellery and knitting. They are displayed on Victorian cast-iron trading stands from the old flower market.

Theatre Royal, Drury Lane

The Theatre Royal, Drury Lane, has a long history. Nell Gwynn, mistress of Charles the Second, once sold oranges to the playgoers. There is also said to be a ghost at the back of the theatre. In Victorian times a bricked up room was found. Inside was a skeleton with a dagger in its ribs.

There is a separate covered market, called the Jubilee Market, held on one side of the Piazza. It sells all kinds of things on weekdays. On Saturdays it sells art and craft work.

Samuel Pepys saw the first Punch and Judy show performed in England in front of Saint Paul's Church, and ever since that time the Piazza has been famous for street theatre. Every day acts of all kinds perform, usually in front of the church. You can see mime artists, jugglers, dancers, buskers and many others. Nearby in Tavistock Street is the Theatrical Museum which opened in 1987.

Street theatre in the Piazza

Trafalgar Square

Before Trafalgar Square was laid out in Victorian times it was the site of the old Royal Mews, or stables. Hunting falcons were once kept there. The Square was named to commemorate Admiral Lord Nelson's naval victory over the French at Trafalgar in 1805. Today it is a place where people meet, and is a site famous for political demonstrations.

Nelson's Column

Landseer modelling one of the lions

The Square's most famous landmark is Nelson's Column. There are four bronze lions around it, made by the artist, Sir Edwin Landseer. They were cast from the cannon of battle-ships. On 21 October each year there is a service under the column to commemorate Nelson.

A few days before Nelson's statue was erected fourteen stonemasons held a dinner on top of the column.

Before the statue was hoisted up it was put on show to the public. It has never come down since; people climb up the column to clean and restore it.

Nelson's statue before it was put on the column

Sights in the Square

George the Fourth's statue

Around the Square there are many statues. One shows George the Fourth on horseback. He chose the pose himself and made it very heroic – he is riding in Roman costume, bareback and without stirrups.

Charles the First's statue

A statue of Charles the First on horseback looks down Whitehall. During the Civil War it was sold to a brazier to melt down. But he hid it in his garden and produced it again when the monarchy returned.

The police box

In a corner of the Square there is a small hollow pillar, built as an observation post for one policeman. It is London's smallest police office. The lamp on top is said to come from Nelson's flagship Victory.

The Imperial length plaque

On the north wall a brass plaque shows the British Imperial standards of length. Mileages from London are traditionally measured from behind Charles the First's statue.

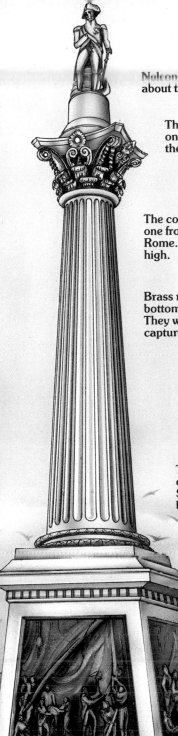

Nelson's statue is over 5m (16ft) high, about three times his real height.

The statue shows Nelson with one arm and one eye. He lost them in battle.

The column is a copy of one from a temple in Rome. It is 51m (167ft) high.

Brass reliefs around the bottom show battle scenes. They were cast from captured French cannon.

Thousands of pigeons congregate in Trafalgar Square. In summer you can buy birdseed to feed them.

The National Gallery (see page 54)

Saint Martin-in-the-Fields

Saint Martin's

The church of Saint Martin in the Fields is on the north-east side of the Square. It was built in 1721, and many wooden churches in America, particularly in New England, are copies of it. It is famous for lunchtime concerts. Nell Gwynn and the furniture maker Thomas Chippendale are buried there.

Eleanor's Cross

Eleanor's Cross

In the nearby Strand, by Charing Cross Station, you can see Eleanor's Cross. The original one was erected by Edward the First in memory of his wife Eleanor. It marked the last resting place of her funeral procession before it reached Westminster Abbey in 1291. Today's cross is a Victorian version.

Celebrations

Every year Norway sends Britain a huge Christmas tree, as thanks for wartime help. It stands in the Square from mid December, when the Ambassador of Norway switches on the lights. Carols are sung around it every evening until Christmas.

On New Year's Eve people go to Trafalgar Square to hear the midnight chimes of Big Ben.

Buckingham Palace

Buckingham Palace is the official home of the Queen. It was rebuilt by John Nash in the early 1800s, and was added to in Victorian times. It is a busy royal office, and state occasions are held there.

Palace life

The Royal Standard

The Queen and Prince Philip stay at the Palace on weekdays. They have rooms on the first floor of the north wing. When the Queen is staying the Royal Standard flag is flown above the central balcony.

About 400 people work at the Palace, including domestic servants, chefs, footmen, cleaners, plumbers, gardeners, chauffeurs, electricians, and two people who look after the 300 clocks. About 80 employees live in the Palace rooms.

Part of the Queen's apartment is a sitting room with an office where she works. Every morning during breakfast bagpipes are played outside her private dining room. Prince Philip has his own office and library.

The Royal Crest appears on British post vans.

The Palace has its own post office and its mail is sent free, because Britain's postal service, the "Royal Mail", is run with the Queen's permission. In the morning lorries deliver fruit and vegetables to the Palace from the royal farms.

The Royal Mews

The Irish State Coach, kept in the Mews

On some weekdays you can visit the Palace Royal Mews, and see the horses and coaches used by royalty, including the Gold State Coach and the glass coach used at royal weddings.

On a visit to the Mews you may see a royal car driving in or out. There are about twenty, mostly Rolls Royces. Instead of licence plates the Queen's official cars show the royal coat of arms.

There are about 600 rooms at the Palace, on three main floors. The large picture below shows the back view that visitors do not normally see.

1 On the third floor there are wardrobe rooms full of the Queen's clothes and jewels. Assistants make sure every outfit is in perfect condition. They are all carefully listed and indexed, and records are kept of the outfits the Queen has worn on every occasion.

The private royal apartments

Queen's private entrance

Swimming pool

4 The 40-acre private garden has its own lake and a stock of pink flamingos. Every year, garden parties are held there, with thousands of guests invited from all walks of life. Sometimes the Queen walks her corgi dogs around the grounds. There is an indoor swimming pool and also a cinema at the Palace.

Pall Mall

Queen Victoria Memorial

2 The royal family stand on the central balcony at the front of the Palace to wave to the crowds on important occasions. Behind this famous balcony is a room decorated with yellow silks and Chinese-style furniture and wallpaper.

The view from behind the balcony

3 The Queen's Gallery is open to the public on most weekdays. It houses paintings, drawings and furniture from the royal collection, including portraits of members of the royal family who have lived at the Palace.

Post office

Kitchens, ballroom and staff quarters

Cinema

State apartments along this side

5 The State Dining Room, with a table for 60 guests.

Some of the grandest rooms in the Palace are the State Apartments, on the first floor of the west wing. They include the White, Green and Blue Drawing Rooms, each decorated to match their names. There is a Music Room, a State Dining Room and a huge ballroom where medals are presented at special ceremonies.

6 Five regiments of Foot Guards from the Household Brigade mount regular guard outside the Palace. The Guard is changed daily in the Palace forecourt when the Queen is in residence. The ceremony lasts for about half an hour.

Changing the Guard

31

London Parks

London has more parkland than almost any other world capital. The Royal Parks featured on the next four pages are the most central.* They belong to the monarch but are open to the public during daylight hours. Besides these there are many smaller local parks, playgrounds and public gardens around London.

The Royal Parks were first used as private royal hunting forests. When they were opened to the public they became fashionable areas to be seen. They were also popular places to hold duels at dawn.

Today the Parks are looked after by hundreds of workers, who tend the gardens and keep the parks clean daily. There are regular police patrols, too, and there is a special police station in the middle of Hyde Park.

There is a variety of wildlife in all the Royal Parks, especially birdlife, which changes with the seasons. There are usually lots of different kinds of duck around the ponds and lakes, and you may see grey squirrels or hedgehogs.

Saint James's Park and Green Park

Saint James's Park and Green Park lie close together, with Buckingham Palace between them. Alongside Saint James's Park runs Pall Mall. Its name comes from an old French type of croquet called *paille maille*. Charles the Second used to have a *paille maille* alley nearby.

● Green Park
▲ Fardel rest
✹ Pall Mall
○ Duck Island
▽ Buckingham Palace
■ Saint James's Park
Whitehall

Park sights

Saint James's Park is famous for the variety of ducks, geese and other birds which live on its lake, including pelicans. On the north bank there are picture tiles to help you identify the different species. Some are very tame and will eat crumbs from your hand.

The fardel rest

Beside Green Park, in Piccadilly, you can see a fardel rest, a high bench set into the pavement. It was made for Victorian porters to rest their bundles on.

Saint James's Park lake, with the government offices of Whitehall in the background

*You can find out about Royal Parks in outer London on pages 42-45.

Hyde Park and Kensington Gardens

Hyde Park was once part of a wild and ancient forest, inhabited by wolves, wild bulls and boar. It was fenced off as a royal deer park in Tudor times, and later opened to the public. Kensington Gardens shares the Serpentine Lake with Hyde Park. The part in Kensington Gardens is called The Long Water.

Things to see and do

There is a tradition to swim in the Serpentine on Christmas Day, however icy the water. At other times you can hire rowing boats. The Round Pond in Kensington Gardens is good for sailing model boats.

The Serpentine

Apsley House

Hyde Park Corner is at the eastern entrance to Hyde Park. In the centre is a triumphal arch dedicated to the Duke of Wellington, who led the British at the Battle of Waterloo. Nearby is his old home, Apsley House, now a Wellington museum.

Peter Pan

By The Long Water there is a bronze statue of Peter Pan. Around its base are fairies, fieldmice and rabbits. In the Kensington playground there is an old treestump called the Elfin Oak, carved with elves and fairies climbing up it.

Kensington Palace Gardens

Several members of today's royal family have apartments at Kensington Palace, in Kensington Gardens. You can walk around the Palace Gardens and visit the State Apartments. There is also an exhibition of uniforms and dresses once worn at Court.

Park events

In November the London to Brighton Car Run starts from Hyde Park.

On royal birthdays gun salutes are fired in Hyde Park.

Every weekend afternoon you can listen to people making speeches at Speakers' Corner, in Hyde Park. Anyone has the right to speak here.

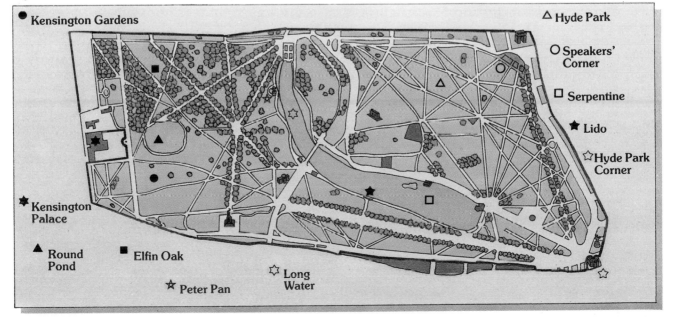

Regent's Park

Regent's Park was originally a royal hunting forest. It was landscaped by John Nash in the 1820s for the Prince Regent (later George the Fourth). He surrounded it with elegant terraced houses, which you can still see today. The Park is the home of London Zoo.

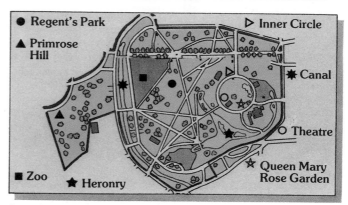

● Regent's Park
▲ Primrose Hill
▷ Inner Circle
✶ Canal
○ Theatre
☆ Queen Mary Rose Garden
■ Zoo
★ Heronry

Around the Park

Inside the Park's Inner Circle is the Queen Mary Rose Garden, full of carefully-tended flower borders and wall roses.

Near Regent's Park is Primrose Hill, once a thieves' hideout. From the top there is a good view of London.

In summer plays are staged at the open-air theatre in the Park, and brass bands sometimes play on the bandstand.

You can hire boats on the lake in the Park. On one of its islands there is a heronry, where herons live and breed.

In the early 1800s canals were built to link the London docks with other parts of the country. Regent's Canal is one of these. It runs through part of Regent's Park, and has been restored so you can walk along it and take narrow-boat trips between Camden Lock and Little Venice.

At Camden Lock there are working lock gates and craft workshops in old canal-side warehouses. Every May there is a canal procession of decorated barges. The best place to see it is at Little Venice.

Regent's Canal

London Zoo

Early days at the Zoo

London Zoo was opened in 1827 by the Zoological Society of London. The first enclosures were built to reflect the places the animals came from. African animals were kept in grass huts and goats lived in a Swiss-style chalet, for instance.

Today there are more ▶ than 8,000 animals in the Zoo. Some are very rare, so are encouraged to breed. Many of the animals were born in the Zoo, or in other zoos around the world.

The giant Panda, a very rare animal in the Zoo.

◀ You can adopt an animal at London Zoo for a year. The cost depends on the animal you choose, and is based on the amount of food it eats in a year. Your name goes on a plaque near the animal's cage.

The elephants and rhinos ▶ have the biggest appetites in the Zoo. An elephant's daily diet consists of hay, grass pellets, cabbage, carrots, apples, potatoes, dates, bread, salt, vitamins and minerals, washed down with 100 litres (26 US gallons).

Zoo sights

The Snowdon Aviary

You can walk through the Snowdon Aviary, where about 150 different species of bird live. They have lots of room to fly freely around inside, and there are cliff-faces, water, trees and bushes to simulate different kinds of bird habitat.

In the Children's Zoo there are all kinds of pets and farm animals, too, such as sheep, miniature pigs and cows. At 3 o'clock each afternoon you can see the cows being milked. The milk is used to feed some of the other Zoo animals.

Every day you can watch animals being fed, for instance penguins, snakes, lions and seals. Around the Zoo there are trays of exhibits you can touch, for instance, you might be able to handle a crocodile skin or a snake skeleton.

A bushbaby in the Moonlight World

In the Moonlight World you can see nocturnal creatures, who sleep during daylight hours and wake up when it is dark. In this building day and night are reversed by artificial light, so that visitors can see the animals awake in the daytime.

In summer a baby elephant walks around the Zoo with its keeper. You can also see the "elephant's workout" at the Elephant House. One of the baby elephants goes through some of its training exercises, and you can help to weigh it.

In summer you can have a ride on a pony, donkey or camel, or in a cart pulled by a South American llama. You can meet some of the small animals and their keepers in a summer afternoon show in the Zoo's Hummingbird Amphitheatre.

More London parks and open spaces

There are lots of other parks and open spaces around London. Many of them have sports areas and playgrounds, and hold annual fairs and festivals. A few are listed below.

⭐ **Alexandra Park:** Lake, paddling pool, adventure playground and animal enclosure.

⭐ **Battersea Park:** Play area and pets' corner. Lots of events, including Easter and May Day celebrations with carnival processions

⭐ **Blackheath:** A fair in summer and a kite display every Easter.

⭐ **Clapham Common:** Ponds, a playground and a bandstand. The Greater London Horse Show is held every August, with all kinds of horse events and traditional craft displays.

⭐ **Crystal Palace Park:** A boating lake, summer children's zoo, Sunday concerts and giant models of dinosaurs.

⭐ **Hampstead Heath:** A huge heath with ponds, some for swimming. A big fun-fair held every summer.

⭐ **Holland Park:** Set in the grounds of a historic house, with an open-air theatre and a playpark.

⭐ **Wimbledon Common:** Large heath, with a pond, ancient earthworks and a windmill.

⭐ **City farms:** There are several around London, set up to show people how a farm runs. You can visit them to see the animals, and sometimes help in the farm work. There is a list on page 62.

Big London museums

Over the next four pages you can find out about the five major public London museums – the British Museum, in Bloomsbury, and the Victoria and Albert, Natural History, Geology and Science Museums, which are all near to each other in Kensington.

Tips for visitors

The major museums are very large, with thousands of exhibits. Below are some useful tips to help get the most out of a visit.

* It is impossible to see everything in one day. Instead you could concentrate on two or three rooms or pick out the most famous exhibits to see.

* At the museum information desks you can often get children's project sheets, which have information and activities based on the displays.

* Special temporary exhibitions are often held. They are advertised in newspapers or on posters.

* At the museum shops you can buy guides, souvenirs and books.

Museum people

Hundreds of people work in the Museums. A few of them are shown below.

Technicians make and mend things around the buildings.

Warders guard exhibits and help visitors.

Curators look after the exhibits and study their origins.

A Director is in charge of each museum.

The British Museum

The British Museum houses ancient objects from many historic civilizations, including ancient Egypt, Greece and Roman Britain. It began in 1759 (see page 9), and was rehoused in its present Greek-style building in Victorian times.

A cut-away picture of the front of the Museum is shown below, and there are descriptions of some of the most famous exhibits on show.

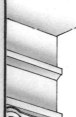

Room 69, Greek and Roman life.

Bookshop

Entrance

Transporting a giant statue

There are many giant statues in the Museum. Some were collected by Victorian archaeologists who discovered the ruins of ancient cities and huge palaces in parts of the Middle East. They were transported to Britain, first by wagon, then by sea.

This picture shows a huge winged lion with a human head being pulled up the Museum steps in 1852. It once guarded a palace in ancient Assyria (now Iraq). It has five legs, so from the front it looks as if it is standing, and from the side as if it is walking.

The Elgin Marbles   Chariot horse

The Elgin Marbles are sculptures from the Greek Parthenon in Athens. They were brought back to Britain in 1802-4 by Lord Elgin. They show the birth of Athena and processions to honour her. According to legend she was born out of the head of the God Zeus, when another God hit him with a hammer to get rid of his headache.

Cat

Man

The Museum is famous for Egyptian mummies, shown on the left. The Egyptians thought that life would continue after death, so they preserved the body for the dead person's spirit to live in. It was buried with treasure, household goods and even servants, to use in the next life.

You can see the mummies of kings, queens and their servants.

The Sutton Hoo treasure comes from the burial site of a seventh century Anglo-Saxon king in Suffolk. He was buried in a complete ship along with a rich treasure hoard to use in the afterlife.

Among the many items on show are drinking horns, beautiful gold buckles and the king's helmet. It has been restored from over five hundred pieces.

Buckle

Helmet

Rooms 37-39, late prehistory of Europe.

Room 47, Renaissance life.

Library

The British Library forms part of the Museum. It contains many original manuscripts of famous books and documents, including Lewis Carroll's Alice in Wonderland and some of the original Beatles' song lyrics.

There is a big collection of fairy tale book illustrations to see, and the beautiful Lindisfarne Gospels. They were made by monks in about 698 AD. Part of the library is a huge circular reading room, where scholars research and study.

The Rosetta Stone, now in the Museum, was the key to understanding ancient Egyptian picture writing, called hieroglyphs. It came from an old wall in the village of Rosetta in Egypt.

Its inscription is repeated in three different types of writing – in hieroglyphs, in another form of Egyptian writing and in Greek. By translating the Greek, scholars were able to work out the hieroglyphs and begin to understand the ancient Egyptian language. The writing tells of battles of the time.

The Natural History Museum

The Natural History Museum houses a huge collection of animal and plant specimens. It is a good example of how things have changed since the major London museums opened in the 1800s, when they had a very scholarly and formal atmosphere. Many of today's displays are designed so that visitors can find out information for themselves and have lots of fun. For instance, there are models to work, and computer games to play.

The Museum building was designed by Alfred Waterhouse. The main hall ceiling is painted with different types of plants, and all over the building there are red pottery (terracotta) mouldings of living and extinct animals and plants.

Ceiling paintings

The Museum's work

A scientist studies a specimen with a microscope.

The Museum is an important research centre. Over 300 scientists carry out detective work on new finds to learn more about how animals and plants function. About 2,500 new plant and animal species are discovered every year, and the Museum keeps a careful record of them all.

Fossils and whales

Blue whale model

The Museum is famous for its fossil collection, and for its reconstructions of huge and fierce prehistoric animals. In the Whale Hall there is a full-scale model of the biggest animal in the modern world, the blue whale. It is over 27m (89ft) long, the length of more than three London double-decker buses.

The Geological Museum

The Geological Museum is a separate section of the Natural History Museum, in its own building. The exhibitions there are designed to help people understand what makes up the Earth – for instance, its rocks, mountains and volcanoes. There are some spectacular special exhibitions to see.

Story of the Earth

The "Story of the Earth Exhibition" is about the way the Earth developed, and the way its geology is still changing. Among the things to see is a working model of a volcanic island being formed. There is also a special floor which shakes to show what it feels like to be in an earthquake.

The earthquake floor

Minerals to touch

The "Treasures of the Earth Exhibition" is about the most important natural substances that come out of the ground, and how they are used in everyday life. Among the displays there are games to play, computers to use, and different kinds of minerals laid out for you to touch.

Precious jewels

The Museum has one of the best gemstone collections in the world. There are over 3,000 on show, both in their natural state and cut for jewellery. The display includes diamonds, rubies and emeralds. You can learn about the rocks in which they are found and the best places to look for them.

The Science Museum

The exhibitions in the Science Museum are designed to help people understand science and technology, past and present. The displays show everyday machines as well as highly developed technology – from ordinary calculators to real spacecraft in the newly developed Space Hall.

Behind the scenes

Museum staff are busy looking after exhibits, and making sure they are clean and undamaged. They keep records and research into scientific history, and sometimes help ordinary people to identify scientific objects which they bring.

Taking part

In a new exhibition called "Launchpad" visitors can work lots of the exhibits themselves. There are also displays to work in the Children's Gallery, such as a real submarine periscope. If you look through it you can see other museum floors.

The periscope

Wellcome Museum

The Wellcome Museum, part of the Science Museum, is about the history of medicine. One floor is filled with realistic scenes depicting medicine through the ages, from a Roman army hospital to a modern operating theatre. There is a nineteenth century chemist's shop, where you can walk in as if you were a customer.

Nineteenth century chemist's shop

The Victoria and Albert Museum (V & A)

The Victoria and Albert Museum, nicknamed the V & A, has Britain's largest collection of decorative arts: tapestries, costumes, jewellery and glassware, for instance. Apart from its permanent collections it holds many temporary shows. It has a very ornate building, shown on the right.

Paintings

The V & A has a collection of paintings by many famous artists. There is a special collection of tiny detailed miniature portraits. The most famous miniature artist was the Elizabethan Nicholas Hilliard. You can see some of his work at the Museum.

An Elizabethan miniature, based on one by Nicholas Hilliard.

The Bed of Ware

The Great Bed of Ware is kept at the V & A. It is a huge oak bed made in 1580, big enough to hold eight people. It was probably made as a sightseeing attraction for an Inn in the town of Ware. By tradition the people who slept in it carved their names on it.

Costume

The Costume Gallery displays clothes from down the ages, such as those shown below. The oldest item is a boy's embroidered shirt from the 1540s. There are also modern clothes by the latest designers and accessories such as hats and shoes.

Other museums and exhibitions

Apart from the major public museums there are many other museums and exhibitions in London, covering all kinds of subjects. Some charge an entrance fee; others are free. A few are shown on these two pages. You can find out about more on pages 61-62.

Madame Tussaud's

Madame Tussaud's, near Baker Street Station, is the world's most famous wax museum. Over 2 million visitors go there every year to see the lifelike wax figures of historical characters, modern stars, statesmen and notorious criminals.

How it began

Madame Tussaud

Marie Tussaud grew up in Paris in the eighteenth century. Her mother was housekeeper to Doctor Philippe Curtius, a famous wax modeller. He specialized in exhibiting models of famous people, and, as his assistant, Marie learned how to make wax figures.

At the outbreak of the French Revolution in 1789 Dr Curtius and his assistant were ordered to make the death masks of many victims executed by guillotine. Some wax heads made from these masks are still on show.

A guillotine on display.

Madame Tussaud made the death masks of the French King Louis the Sixteenth and Queen Marie Antoinette. Their wax heads are still on display, together with the actual guillotine blade used to execute them.

Models of Louis and Marie Antoinette.

Making wax figures

Today famous people give special sittings for sculptors from Madame Tussaud's. It takes about 3 months to complete a wax model, as shown below.

1 The clay body is modelled on a wire frame.

2 Plaster moulds are made of the clay head and body. The head mould is filled with molten wax. The body mould is lined with fibreglass and then chipped away.

3 The cooled wax head is fitted with glass eyes and real hair, which is washed and styled.

4 The model is painted with water-colour and make-up.

Special exhibits

There are some wax visitors dotted around the displays, and many people are fooled by them because they look so real. There are many historical figures, too, for instance Henry the Eighth and his six wives, shown below.

The Battle of Trafalgar exhibit shows scenes inside Nelson's flagship, HMS Victory, at the height of battle. The noise of the guns was recorded on board the original ship, now moored at Portsmouth.

Another famous display is in the Chamber of Horrors, where there are models of some of the most notorious criminals of history.

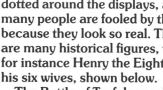

Jane Seymour (died)

Catherine Howard (beheaded)

Anne Boleyn (beheaded)

Henry the Eighth

Anne of Cleves (divorced)

Catherine Parr (outlived the King)

Catherine of Aragon (divorced)

The Planetarium

The London Planetarium, next to Madame Tussaud's, houses astronomical displays. Under its large dome visitors can see a spectacular Star Show – a projection of the Universe accompanied by a commentary and special effects.

Planetarium Projector

A model of Galileo, who discovered new facts about the solar system in the seventeenth century.

The Planetarium exhibition shows how ideas about astronomy have developed over thousands of years, with wax models of the most important astronomers placed in settings representing their discoveries.

During a Star Show vistors sit on reclining seats to watch the ceiling of the Planetarium dome transform into the night sky, with the Sun, planets, moons and nearly 9,000 stars.

The images are created by a large and complicated Zeiss Planetarium Projector. It can re-create the night sky, as seen from any place on Earth, and at any time through history.

The Commonwealth Institute

At the Commonwealth Institute, in Kensington High Street, you can find out about life in the countries of the Commonwealth, a group of 49 nations covering a quarter of the world's land. Each country has a display on its geography, products and life.

Every year in March, on Commonwealth Day, the Institute has a big celebration, when children let off lots of coloured balloons symbolizing peace and hope for the coming year.

The Music Festival

There are always lots of things going on at the Institute, with many activity days, festivals and sometimes storytelling sessions. Every summer a traditional dance and music festival is held in nearby Holland Park.

Museum of Mankind

The Museum of Mankind has a series of exhibitions showing life in non-western societies, both ancient and modern. You can see the homes, costumes, weapons, statues and carvings of many peoples, from Amazonian Indians to African tribespeople.

A head-dress from Equador

Beetle wing cases

Masks and costumes

There are many different kinds of masks and costumes on show. Some are worn to give the wearer the powers of the animal, bird or demon the masks represent. They are often made from leaves and brightly coloured bird feathers, and painted or decorated with beads.

A North American Indian mask

41

Outer London

There are many places to visit and things to do on the outskirts of Greater London, and lots of trips you can take outside the capital. You can find out about some of them on the next four pages.

Hampton Court

Hampton Court was built in the early 1500s for Cardinal Wolsey, Henry the Eighth's chief minister. He lived a life of luxury there until he displeased the king by not arranging a quick divorce from the king's first wife, Catherine of Aragon. To please King Henry,

Great Gatehouse
The King's beasts

Cardinal Wolsey

Cardinal Wolsey presented him with Hampton Court, but it did not do any good. The Cardinal was accused of high treason. He fell ill and died on his way to London to face the charges.

Henry moved in, with his new wife Anne Boleyn. You can see his symbol, the Tudor rose, around old parts of the Palace. In front of the Great Gatehouse there are statues of the "King's beasts", animals representing royalty. They are replicas of Henry's originals.

In 1689 King William and Queen Mary commissioned Sir Christopher Wren to rebuild parts of the Palace. They liked Hampton Court because it was out in the country, away from London. Wren's elegant royal apartments are open to the public.

Things to see

On Anne Boleyn's Gate there is an astronomical clock. It tells the hours, the month, the day of the month, the zodiac sign, the day of the year, the moon phases and Thames high tide time.

Real tennis

Henry enjoyed playing "real tennis", and built an indoor tennis court, still used today. In real tennis the ball is solid, and the players bounce it off the court walls and over the net.

The maze

One of Hampton Court's most famous features is its 300-year-old maze. There is also a great vine, planted in 1769. It has a huge stem about 2m (6.4ft) across, and still has a good yearly grape crop.

The Great Hall

Henry built the Great Hall where he held grand feasts. He was so impatient to finish it that his men worked through the night by candlelight. There is a stone square at one end where fires were lit.

The palace ghost

Catherine Howard was Henry the Eighth's fifth wife. She was condemned for infidelity and sentenced to execution at the Tower of London. The story says that she tried to make one last appeal to the King before she was taken away from Hampton Court.

She escaped from her guards and reached a doorway leading to the chapel where Henry was at Mass. There she was caught and carried away screaming. Her ghost is said to appear at night at the door and then, with screams, she disappears. This area of the Palace is called the Haunted Gallery.

Richmond Park

There was once a medieval royal palace at Richmond. It was called "Shene", meaning a beautiful shining place. Henry the Seventh rebuilt the old palace. He was the Earl of Richmond (in Yorkshire), and he gave the palace site its present name. But all that is now left of the royal home is an old gatehouse on Richmond Green, and the name of Sheen, a district nearby.

Henry the Eighth's mound

White Lodge

Richmond Park is 10 sq.km (4 sq. miles) of countryside. It was used for centuries as a royal hunting area. In the Park there is a hillock called "Henry the Eighth mound". It may have been the place where the King stood to shoot deer.

After the Civil War the land was given to the City of London in return for helping Cromwell. But it was returned to the Crown later. In the Park you can see the White Lodge, built as a shooting lodge for George the Second.

About 600 red and fallow deer still roam freely in the Park. The rutting season is in the autumn, when the stags roar out challenges and fight each other for mates. It is best to keep away from the deer at this time.

Kew Gardens

Kew Gardens is the home of the Royal Botanical Society. It has the most famous collection of plants and flowers in the world, with about 30,000 varieties of plants and trees, and seven million dried specimens from around the world. Many of them are on display.

The glass-houses

As well as being a beautiful place to visit Kew is also an important scientific centre. Behind the scenes lots of botanical research work is done on newly discovered plants, and on the best ways of cultivating flowers and growing crops world-wide.

The plants are either in the open or in huge glass hot-houses, once the biggest greenhouses in existence. They house strange and exotic plants from many countries, including fly-catching plants, and huge palm trees reaching to the roof.

The pagoda

Princess Augusta, mother of George the Third, began the Gardens. She had the famous 10-storey Chinese-style pagoda built, that still stands in the grounds. In the gardens you can visit Kew Palace, a house used by George the Third.

The Temperate House at Kew

Greenwich

Greenwich is famous as the centre of the world's time system. It is also the home of the National Maritime Museum, one of the largest nautical museums in the world, and is the mooring place of the Cutty Sark and Gipsy Moth IV, two historic British craft. Also at Greenwich is the Royal Naval College, designed by Sir Christopher Wren as a seaman's hospital.

The National Maritime Museum

The Museum shows British sailing history from ancient times to the present day. There are lots of detailed ship models, paintings, uniforms, weapons, and displays on every kind of boat, and on famous voyages.

The Maritime Museum

Nelson's uniform

There is a gallery devoted to Britain's greatest Admiral, Lord Nelson. You can see how Nelson lived on board ship, and the bloodstained uniform he was wearing when he was shot at Trafalgar by a French sniper.

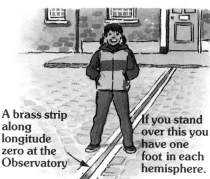

A brass strip along longitude zero at the Observatory

If you stand over this you have one foot in each hemisphere.

The Museum also runs the Old Royal Observatory, on a hill overlooking Greenwich Park. It is the home of Greenwich Mean Time.

The line between the world's eastern and western hemispheres, "longitude zero", runs through Greenwich, and time in different countries throughout the world is worked out based on this line.

In the Observatory you can see lots of astronomical and time-measuring instruments on display, including telescopes, clocks and sun-dials.

The red "time ball"

On the roof there is a red "time ball". It rises to the top of its mast and drops at exactly 1pm every day, controlled by a 24-hour clock on the wall below. It was once used as a time signal for ships on the Thames.

Cutty Sark

You can go on board the Cutty Sark, in dry dock at Greenwich. She is the last remaining sailing "clipper", launched in 1869. To go "at a clip" meant to travel fast, which the Cutty Sark was designed to do. First she brought home tea from China. Later she collected wool from Australia.

Near the Cutty Sark you can visit Gipsy Moth IV, the boat in which Sir Francis Chichester made the first single-handed voyage around the world in 1966-7, in order to beat the records set by the old sailing clippers. It took him 274 days. On his return he was knighted by the Queen.

Greenwich Park

Greenwich Park has been in use for centuries. There are ancient burial mounds there, and the remains of a Roman villa were found. There is a playground, gardens, a lake and an enclosure for fallow deer.

Queen Elizabeth's Oak

There is a dead oak tree in the Park called Queen Elizabeth's Oak. By tradition Henry the Eighth danced around the tree with Anne Boleyn, and in its hollow trunk Elizabeth the First once had tea.

The Thames Barrier

The Thames Barrier

The Thames Barrier is the world's largest movable flood barrier, and London's main flood defence. It has huge steel gates, supported between concrete piers covered with curved roofs. When raised the main flood gates stand as high as five-storey houses. You can take a boat trip round the barrier, and see working models at the Visitor Centre.

Syon Park

Things to see in Syon Park

In Syon Park you can see exotic jungle plants in the Great Conservatory. You can also visit the Brit Koi Aquatic Centre where some fish grow to be over 60cm (2ft) long. The London Butterfly House is in the Park grounds. Here you can go on a "butterfly safari" through the tropical greenhouse gardens, where butterflies from around the world fly freely.

Epping Forest

Museum

Epping Forest was once part of a vast and ancient woodland covering most of southern England. It has over a hundred ponds and lakes, and the animal life includes foxes, stoats, rabbits and weasels, as well as local cows and horses allowed to graze on the land by ancient right. The Epping Forest Museum has displays on the forest life through history.

Whipsnade and Chessington

Whipsnade Zoo

At Whipsnade Zoo you can see some of the world's largest and rarest animals, including tigers and white rhinos. A small railway runs through the Park in summer, and you can sometimes see lions, tigers and penguins being fed. Another zoo to visit is Chessington, which has its own circus as well as lots of animals.

Windsor Castle

Windsor Castle was first begun by William the Conqueror, and is the largest inhabited castle in the world. Kings and queens have lived there for 900 years and many are buried in Saint George's Chapel in the grounds. There was a fire at the castle in 1992 and some of the buildings were destroyed, but you can still visit the State Apartments.

The Queen often spends her weekends at Windsor Castle and walks in nearby Windsor Great Park.

Windsor Castle

Transport

London has the largest public transport network in the world. On average, the buses and Underground tube trains carry about 5.5. million people, and travel over 800,000 km (497,000 miles) each day. London Regional Transport has responsibility for the buses and the Underground system.

London transport symbol

UNDERGROUND

Underground symbol

The London Underground

The world's first Underground line opened between Baker Street and the City in 1863 (see page 10). There are now 273 London Underground stations in use, along with tracks covering 404km (250 miles). The system is often called "the tube".

You can get free Underground maps from Underground ticket offices, and they are displayed around the stations. There are nine Underground lines, each one named and given its own colour or black and white pattern on the map, as shown on the right.

Victoria	Central	Circle
District	Metropolitan	Northern
Bakerloo	Piccadilly	Jubilee

Inside a station

Underground stations have complicated tunnel networks, such as the one the right. Apart from the train routes, tunnels need to be built for lifts, escalators, emergency exits, ventilation fans and pedestrian walkways between the different tracks.

A tunnel built near the surface

Early Underground tunnels were built near the surface, by the "cut and cover" method: digging a trench, building a tunnel in it, and then covering it over.

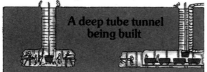

A deep tube tunnel being built

The term "tube" really applies to the deep tunnels built in this century. Deep vertical shafts are dug along the route, and then joined together horizontally, reinforced with a protective shield.

A typical Underground station layout

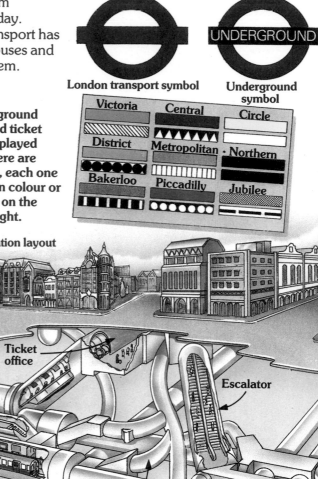

Ventilation shaft

Ticket office

Stairs

Escalator

Tube train

Connecting passage

Platform

Underground facts

Mice and rats live in the train tunnels, feeding on the rubbish they pick up. You can sometimes see them along the tracks.

The Lost Property Office received 106,000 items in 1991/92. There were approximately 11,000 umbrellas.

The tiles at Baker Street Station feature the fictional detective Sherlock Holmes, who lived at 221B Baker Street (see page 55).

On the buses

The first omnibus

The first London bus started running in 1829, between Paddington and the City. It was a horse-drawn coach called an "omnibus", meaning "for all".

An early motor bus

In the early 1900s the first motorized buses were introduced. Today's London double-deckers are the result of many years' technical development.

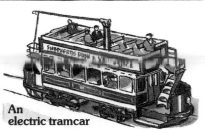

An electric tramcar

In the late nineteenth century trams became popular. They were pulled by horses along special tracks. Later, electric trams and trolleybuses were used.

A troop-carrying bus

London buses were used in both World Wars. During World War One they took troops to the front. You can see one nicknamed "Ole Bill", at the Imperial War Museum.

A London double-decker

British Rail

British Rail (BR) runs overground train services from London to the suburbs and to all parts of Britain. There are 12 main London stations run by BR. Each serves one particular part of the country.

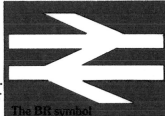

The BR symbol

London taxi cabs

The word "cab" comes from a kind of horse-drawn carriage once used in London, called a "cabriolet". Today's London taxi cabs are usually black, sometimes decorated with advertising slogans. Before drivers can get a taxi licence they have to qualify by memorizing hundreds of time-saving routes and taking tests on them. These tests are called "The Knowledge" and take about two years.

In the air

Heathrow and Gatwick are the two major airports serving the London area. Both of them have viewing decks for spectators, where you can watch planes taking off and landing.

The London Transport Museum

Inside the Museum

The London Transport Museum, in Covent Garden, has displays on the history of transport in the capital, and lots of restored trams, buses and Underground trains which you can board. You can see a replica of the original omnibus, and operate the controls of a modern bus, an Underground train and a tram.

Shopping

London is a famous shopping centre, where you can buy virtually anything. Just a few of its many thousands of shopping sites are shown on these pages.

Harrods

Harrods, shown on the right, is the largest department store in Europe. One of its mottoes is that it sells everything. What it doesn't have it will order, and deliver to anywhere in the world.

Underneath the store there are acres of stockrooms. The store gets its water from its own wells 76m (249ft) below the ground, where there is a tributary of the Thames.

Up in the roof there are painters' and carpenters' shops and an engineers' office with the lift controls. The escalators cover about 68,453km (42,509 miles) a year, nearly twice the distance around the world.

The Harrods colours are green with special gold lettering. Even its carpets are green, patterned with "H" letters.

There are 230 selling departments in Harrods, including its famous food halls, selling every imaginable type of food.

There are 4,000 Harrods staff, and 6,000 for the Christmas sales. The record taking for a day is 7 million pounds, during a sale in January 1987.

Famous shops

Millions of people come every year to shop in London's West End (see page 13). Some of its most famous and popular shops and shopping streets are shown below.

The Burlington Arcade dates from 1818. It is patrolled by guards called beadles. They uphold its old bye-laws – no whistling, singing or hurrying.

Burlington Arcade

Oxford Street and Regent Street are famous for their spectacular illuminated decorations, hung high-up across the streets at Christmas time.

Christmas lights

Liberty's is famous for its fabrics. Part of its 1924 building is timbered like a Tudor house. On the clock outside Saint George chases a dragon every 15 minutes.

Liberty's

Hamleys shop window

Hamleys is the world's largest toy shop. It has six floors filled with toys of all kinds, including dolls, games and models. You can see working mechanical toys around the store.

Fortnum and Mason's sweet counter

Fortnum and Mason sells luxury food, and runs a world-wide delivery service. In the 1800s it sent food parcels to Florence Nightingale in the Crimea, and to the first African expeditions.

January sales

Many London shops have January sales, when they reduce the price of goods. Some people camp on the pavement outside the stores so as to get the best bargains on the opening day.

Markets

There are dozens of London markets. They are always hectic and colourful, and even if you don't buy anything it is worth going along to sample the lively atmosphere. Wholesale markets sell goods to other tradespeople and shopkeepers for resale. They are busy very early in the morning, and by about 9am are usually over. Retail street markets sell to the public, and open during the day.

Wholesale markets

You cannot buy small quantities of things at these markets, but they provide an unusual spectacle if you get up early enough.

New Covent Garden Market, 3am to 11am. A fruit, vegetable and flower market. The original Covent Garden is shown on page 26.

Billingsgate Market, 5am to 8am. A huge fish market. Some of the market porters wear "bobbing" hats made of thick leather and wood, with flat tops for carrying boxes.

Bobbing hat

Billingsgate

Smithfield Market, 5am to 9am. One of the largest wholesale meat markets in the world. Markets have been held here for centuries and medieval fairs and tournaments were once held here, too.

Spitalfields Market, 5.30am to 9am. A fruit and vegetable market on the site of a Roman burial ground. Underneath the market there are big storage rooms where bananas are kept to ripen.

Ordinary street markets

Portobello Market (open Sat). There are over 2,000 stalls here, specializing in antiques

Brixton Market (open Mon-Sat). A daily market with a West Indian atmosphere. Unusual Caribbean-style fruit and vegetables are on sale.

Leadenhall Market (open Mon-Fri). Samuel Pepys wrote about this market in his diary, where he records that he bought a leg of beef for sixpence. It still sells meat, poultry and vegetables

Petticoat Lane (open Sun). This market got its name in the 1600s, when clothes sellers congregated there. Its stalls still sell clothes.

Berwick Street Market (open Mon-Sat). A lively fruit and vegetable market, shown below. It is held in the heart of Soho.

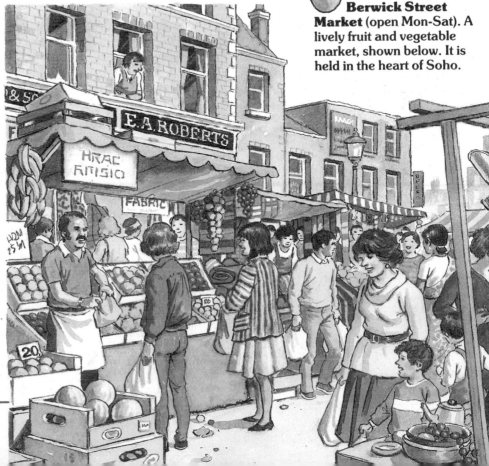

People and places

These pages are about London people and objects you can look out for on the capital's streets.

London Police

The Metropolitan Police force patrol London. They wear blue uniforms and white shirts, and some wear tall helmets, developed from the top hats worn by early policemen.

Two nicknames for British police, "bobbies" and "Peelers", come from the founder of the "Met" Police, Sir Robert Peel.

The Metropolitan Police Thames Division patrols the river in speedboats. They are the oldest uniformed police force in the world, having begun nearly 200 years ago. Their floating police station is by Waterloo Bridge. The City of London has its own police force. They have their own special uniform, shown on the right.

"Met" Constable   City Policewoman   City Policeman

Look out for...

Judges. They wear wigs and knee breeches in a 1700s style. You can see them in early October, when they attend a service at Westminster Abbey.

Traffic wardens. They walk around checking for illegal parking. They wear black uniforms and hats with yellow bands.

Chelsea Pensioners. Old soldiers who live at the Royal Hospital, Chelsea. They wear a scarlet uniform and black hat in the style of the 1700s.

Newspaper sellers. They sell the capital's evening newspapers. They write the news headline on a board by their stall.

Doormen. They stand outside London's exclusive hotels and shops wearing splendid uniforms, hailing taxis and opening doors for guests.

City gents. Some City workers wear bowler hats. They were first designed for gamekeepers, as protection from branches.

Pearly families

Successful Victorian street pedlars called themselves "costermongers". They developed the famous cockney rhyming slang, which replaces words with others that rhyme. There are some examples on page 63.

Costermongers

The Victorian costermongers chose their own leaders to look after their interests. As a mark of authority these leaders wore two rows of pearl buttons on their hats, and became known as the first Pearly Kings. Eventually they began to wear a costume covered in pearl buttons from head to toe, and they still do so today.

The title of Pearly King is passed down in the family, and there are Pearly Queens, Princes and Princesses, too. They now spend their free time collecting for charity, and they have become a famous London institution.

A Pearly King and Queen

Out in the street

Look out for the things below in London's streets

London phone boxes are normally plain red or yellow, but there are unusual Chinese-style ones in Soho. They have pagoda roofs.

Look out for elaborate cast-iron street lamps and benches. For instance, the lamps along the Embankment have dolphins around them.

London's gas lamps were once lit by hand. Only one lamplighter is left. He lights the lamps around the Temple area every evening.

Commemorative plaques are displayed on hundreds of London houses where famous people lived. They are blue with white lettering.

There are over 7,000 public houses ("pubs") in London. Some give their names to their district, for instance "The Angel" at Angel Islington.

The first bollards in London pavements were made from ship's cannon, with the top blocked with a cannon ball. There are still some around.

On the clock outside Fortnum and Mason's shop, in Piccadilly, the figures of Mr Fortnum and Mr Mason come out and bow on the hour.

There is a complicated clock outside the Swiss Centre, Leicester Square. At 12am, 6pm, and 8pm, it plays a long selection of tunes.

Some London houses

In the eighteenth century a standard pattern of town house appeared – tall and three windows wide. The doorways of these houses are usually arched, with a window above called a fanlight.

There are over 800 London streets called "Mews". Most of them were once stable areas, and the attractive cottage-style houses lining them are usually converted servant's quarters.

Roof gables

The picture above shows a typical street of Edwardian houses in a London suburb, first built for middle-class commuters. They usually have long roof gables and bay windows.

Some people live in houseboats on the Thames. The boats are often attractively painted, and decorated with plant pots and trellises. A good place to see them is at Chelsea Wharf.

Many modern blocks of flats have been built for the capital's large population. Thousands of City residents live in the tower blocks and apartment terraces of the Barbican Centre, shown above.

London's most famous address is No.10 Downing Street, the home of British Prime Ministers since 1731. The street is named after the American Sir George Downing, who laid it out.

Traditions and festivals

There are many regular London festivals, celebrations and traditional events. These include State occasions and ceremonial processions, colourful ethnic festivals and strange traditions carried on from ancient times. You can find out about a few of the events on these two pages.*

Ceremonial occasions

Mounting of the Guard. At 10.30 each morning the Queen's Life Guard ride from their barracks in Knightsbridge, through Hyde Park, to Horse Guards' Arch off Whitehall, where they go on duty at 11am.

Beating Retreat. In late May/early June, the massed bands of the Household Division "beat retreat" on Horse Guards' Parade. The procession includes specially trained drum horses carrying big solid silver kettle drums.

Trooping the Colour. This June ceremony celebrates the Queen's official birthday. She leads the procession on horseback to Horse Guards' Parade, where the Colour (the regimental flag) is trooped.

Trooping the Colour

London traditions

There are lots of traditional celebrations unique to London, often based on historical events and ancient practices. You can go along and see some of them. A few are listed below.

Beating the bounds

Commemoration of John Stow (see page 7). John Stow's memorial at Saint Andrew's Undershaft shows him with a real quill pen. In a special yearly service the Lord Mayor replaces the old pen with a new one.

Beating the Bounds. People once learned village boundaries by going on an annual procession called "beating the bounds". Every third year in June the ancient boundaries are still beaten around the Tower of London.

There is a big procession of Beefeaters, clergy and choirboys. At every old boundary mark the Chief Warder shouts out "Whack it boys, whack it!", and the children in the procession beat the marks with willow sticks.

Cart marking. In August City of London street traders gather at the Guildhall Yard, to get their carts marked with the City Arms and a brass number plate.

The Lion Sermon. In October, at St Katherine Cree Church, you can hear the Lion Sermon in memory of a Mayor saved from a lion in Arabia.

Pearly Festival. In September the Pearly harvest festival is held at Saint Martin-in-the-Fields. You can see all the Pearly families outside after the service.

Special British customs

Many old British traditions are celebrated in London as well as other parts of the country.

A fireworks display

Guy Fawkes Night. On the fifth of November people celebrate the discovery of the Gunpowder Plot (see page 16). There are organized bonfires and firework displays around London.

Druids on Tower Hill

Druid festivals. Members of the ancient Celtic Druid religion still celebrate some of Britain's most ancient festivals. In March they gather on Tower Hill, to celebrate the Spring Equinox.

Pancake Greaze

Pancake Day. This is held on Shrove Tuesday, which falls in February or March. Pancake Greaze is held at Westminster School. The school chef tosses a pancake over a high bar and as it falls a group of boys fight for the pieces. The boy with the heaviest piece wins a prize.

River events

Swan-upping

Swan-upping. In July the Queen's men and members of the Dyers and Vintners Livery Companies row up the river, picking up cygnets and marking them harmlessly with beak nicks to show who they belong to.

A winner of Dogget's coat and badge   The race umpire, a former winner

Doggett's Coat and Badge Race. In August six Thames boatmen row between London Bridge and Chelsea. The winner gets a scarlet coat with a huge silver badge on one arm. Thomas Doggett set up the race in 1715.

Oxford and Cambridge Boat Race. At Easter the university teams compete between Putney and Mortlake. The blades of the team oars are painted in the university colours, light blue for Cambridge, dark blue for Oxford.

Chinese New Year

The Chinese New Year falls on the first day of the lunar calendar, in January or February. On the nearest weekend there are lively celebrations in Chinatown, Soho.

The streets are brightly decorated and there is a colourful procession led by a model of a dancing lion, who frightens away evil spirits. Red packets full of money are hung outside houses to attract the lion and drive away bad luck.

Art and theatre

There are art galleries all around London, housing lots of valuable works of art. The most famous are shown below.

The National Gallery has one of ▶ the biggest picture collections in the world. A good way to understand them is to get a children's activity sheet from the information desk. These are based on fun themes, such as "Monsters", with questions based on particular pictures.

Inside the National Gallery

The Tate Gallery

The Royal Academy holds a huge ▶ exhibition of over 12,000 pictures from May to August. Anyone can enter, and thousands of people send their works along for selection. They are judged by a panel of artists, and about one in ten get through to the exhibition.

◀ The Tate Gallery houses a special collection of historic British paintings, and lots of exciting and surprising modern exhibits from around the world, including unusual sculptures and abstract paintings. During school holidays there are children's quizzes and trails.

Practical places

Many local arts and community centres put on plays and workshops for children, when you can have a go at acting, dancing and all kinds of crafts. There are some useful addresses on page 62.

London Brass-Rubbing Centre. A big collection of replica English church brasses to rub. For a small charge you can get all the materials.

The Bethnal Green Museum of Childhood. The Bethnal Green Museum runs practical days on things like puppet and toy-making, based on its collection of toys through the ages.

Theatres

Some London theatres put on plays for young people. A few are listed below.

The Molecule Theatre. The Molecule Theatre puts on lively fantasy plays, which help to explain simple scientific principles in a fun way.

The Polka Children's Theatre. Lots of exciting and funny shows, using puppets, toys and magic. There are also puppet, music, clowning and storytelling sessions.

The Unicorn Theatre for Children. The Unicorn puts on plays full of adventure, magic and comedy. There are all kinds of theatre workshops to join in, too, where you can have a go at acting and scene-painting.

The Royal Shakespeare Company and the National Theatre. Both run backstage trips to see rehearsal rooms, scenery workshops and backstage equipment.

The Little Angel Marionette Theatre. This theatre puts on a wide range of plays and shows with live magicians. There is just so much to see.

London theatres put on lively pantomimes at Christmas, plays based on fairytale themes. They are performed by famous stars, and the audience is often asked to join in. Traditional pantomimes include Cinderella, Jack and the Beanstalk, and Aladdin and his lamp.

A scene from Aladdin

Legendary Londoners

Many real and fictional characters have been associated with London through the centuries.

On this page you can find out more about some of London's most famous names.

Sherlock Holmes

Sherlock Holmes was a fictional Victorian detective created by Sir Arthur Conan Doyle in the 1880's. Most of the stories are written in the voice of Doctor Watson, Holmes' friend and assistant crime-solver.

Sherlock Holmes

Many of the stories are set partly in London, and include fictional characters from its criminal underworld. In the novels, Sherlock Holmes lived at 221B Baker Street, now a Building Society.

Charles Dickens

As a young man the Victorian novelist Charles Dickens worked as a reporter in the law courts and at the Houses of Parliament. He got to know the city well, and describes many Londoners and districts in all his major books.

A scene from "Oliver Twist" about young pickpockets in a London slum.

One of Dickens' homes, 48 Doughty Street in Bloomsbury, is open as a Dickens Museum. He lived there from 1837 to 1839, when he wrote Pickwick Papers, Oliver Twist and Nicholas Nickleby.

Jack the Ripper

Jack the Ripper was a notorious murderer who terrorized London in 1888. He prowled the slums of the Spitalfields area, and committed five murders in ten weeks, despite 600 policemen being sent to catch him.

Jack the Ripper prowls the streets.

The identity of the Ripper is one of the great unsolved crime mysteries, although there are many theories about him. You can go on "Jack the Ripper" walks around London, to see the scenes of his crimes.

Dick Whittington

Dick Whittington is one of London's best-known legends. The story goes that Dick Whittington was a poor country boy, who walked to London to seek his fortune, carrying his few belongings in a bundle on the end of a stick.

Dick got a job as a cook's boy in the house of a merchant, Mr. Fitzwarren, and he bought a cat to help him keep down the mice in his tiny room. But he was treated badly by the cook, and eventually decided to go home.

As Dick got to the edge of London the Bow bells rang out, and what they said persuaded Dick to return: "Turn again Dick Whittington, Thrice Lord Mayor of London". Meanwhile Dick's cat had gone on-board a ship.

The cat was a good ratcatcher, and killed a plague of rats in a distant country. The Emperor bought the cat for a fortune, which was returned to Dick. He became a wealthy merchant, and was Lord Mayor of London three times.

There was a real Dick Whittington, who became Lord Mayor three times in the early 1400s. He came to London and set up as a merchant. The cat legend may come from the coal barges called "cats", which Whittington owned.

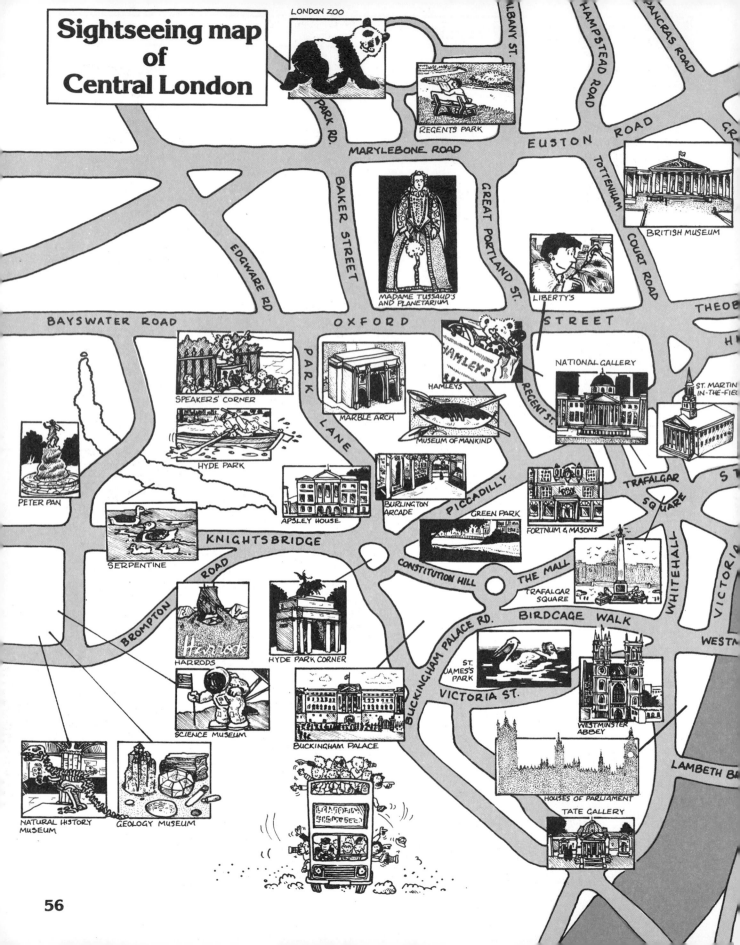

Sightseeing map of Central London

LONDON ZOO

REGENTS PARK

ALBANY ST.

HAMPSTEAD ROAD

PANCRAS ROAD

PARK RD.

MARYLEBONE ROAD

EUSTON ROAD

BAKER STREET

GREAT PORTLAND ST.

TOTTENHAM COURT ROAD

GR

BRITISH MUSEUM

EDGWARE RD.

MADAME TUSSAUD'S AND PLANETARIUM

LIBERTY'S

THEOB

BAYSWATER ROAD

OXFORD STREET

H

SPEAKERS' CORNER

MARBLE ARCH

HAMLEYS

NATIONAL GALLERY

ST. MARTIN IN-THE-FIE

PARK LANE

MUSEUM OF MANKIND

HYDE PARK

REGENT ST.

PETER PAN

APSLEY HOUSE

BURLINGTON ARCADE

PICCADILLY

GREEN PARK

FORTNUM & MASONS

TRAFALGAR SQUARE

ST

SERPENTINE

KNIGHTSBRIDGE

CONSTITUTION HILL

THE MALL

TRAFALGAR SQUARE

WHITEHALL

BROMPTON ROAD

HARRODS

HYDE PARK CORNER

BUCKINGHAM PALACE RD.

BIRDCAGE WALK

WESTM

SCIENCE MUSEUM

BUCKINGHAM PALACE

ST. JAMES'S PARK

VICTORIA ST.

WESTMINSTER ABBEY

VICTORIA

LAMBETH BR

NATURAL HISTORY MUSEUM

GEOLOGY MUSEUM

HOUSES OF PARLIAMENT

TATE GALLERY

The map below shows the general position of most of the main London sights so far mentioned in this book, together with a few of the major roads to look out for if you are travelling from place to place. If you want to go by tube you can find out which underground stop to choose under each entry in the gazetteer over the next few pages. You can get a map of bus routes from any Travel Centre.

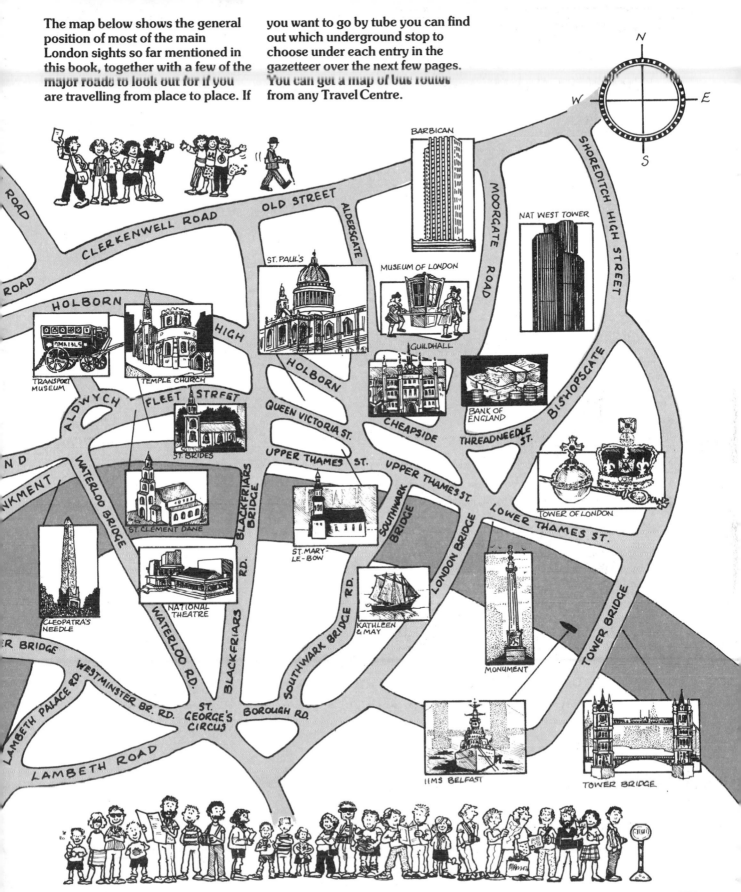

Visitor's guide

The following pages are full of useful information. The addresses and opening times of all the places mentioned in this book are shown, plus tips on other things to see.

★ Remember that some places may be closed on bank holidays. Most are closed for Christmas.

★ It is a good idea to check opening times before going on a visit, because these are often changed.

★ To check a London number while outside London ring 142 (Directory Enquiries). From London ring 192.

Getting around

London is divided into postal districts, each with a postal code based on direction from the middle of London. For instance, SW means South-West, WC means West-Central and E means East. As well as initials, each code has a number. For instance, the code for the area around the Houses of Parliament is SW1. The higher the number the farther away the place will be from the middle of the capital. You can tell from this code the general position of a place in London. You can buy an "A to Z", which contains detailed maps of every part of the capital. At the back there is a street index, with a map reference, as shown below.

Street name → **Garrick St. WC2 – 3E 60d** ← Map reference
District code ↗ ↖ Page reference

Travel passes

For British Rail information you can go to the British Rail Travel Centre, 12 Regent Street, SW1. The major stations have travel centres, too. British Rail is referred to as BR in this Guide's entries.

You can obtain transport information and buy special visitor's travel passes from underground stations, or at any one of the Information Centres at **Charing Cross, Euston, Heathrow, King's Cross, Oxford Circus, Piccadilly Circus, St James's Park** or **Victoria**.

Visiting details

P11 Museum of London, London Wall, EC2. ☎ 071 600 3699. Open Tues-Sat 10am-6pm. Sun 12am-6pm. Closed Mon , Jan 1, Dec 25-26. Tube: Barbican.

P14/15 Westminster Abbey, Westminster, W1. ☎ 071 222 5152. Nave and Cloisters open Mon-Sat 8am-6pm (Wed until 7.45pm). Royal Chapel, Poet's Corner, Choir, Statesman's Aisle open Mon-Fri 9am-4.45pm. Last Admission 4pm. Sat 9am-2.45pm, 3.45pm-5.45pm. Admission charge for Royal Chapel. Brass Rubbing Centre open Mon-Sat 9am-5pm. Fee charged for brass rubbing. Tube: Westminster.

P16/17 Houses of Parliament, Westminster, SW1. ☎ 071 219 4272. Public Gallery open when House is sitting, Mon-Thurs from 2.30pm (closed bank holidays) – queue outside St Stephen's entrance. Other visits through application to your local M.P. Opening of Parliament – beginning of November (date varies). Tube: Westminster.

P18/19 Lord Mayor's Show, second Saturday in November – late morning until early afternoon. From Guildhall via Strand to Law Courts.

Guildhall, Basinghall Street, EC2. ☎ 071 606 3030. Open 10am-5pm. Sun 2pm-5pm. Closed for special functions. Tube: St Paul's.
St Mary-le-Bow, Cheapside, EC2. ☎ 071 248 5139. Tube: Mansion House.
St Bride's, Fleet Street, EC4. ☎ 071 353 1301. Tube: Blackfriars.
St Clement Dane, Strand WC2. ☎ 071 242 8282. Tube: Aldwych.
Temple Church, Inner Temple, EC4. ☎ 071 353 1736. Tube: Temple.
Stock Exchange, Old Broad Street, EC2. ☎ 071 588 2355. Tube: Bank.

Presentation of Knollys Rose – held at the end of June. ☎ Guildhall – 071 606 3030 for date. Procession is from All Hallows-by-the-Tower to the Mansion House.

Boar's Head procession – early December. ☎ Guildhall – 071 606 3030 for date. Procession from Smithfield College of the Distributive Trades to Mansion House.
The Monument, Monument Street, EC4. ☎ 071 626 2717. Open Mon-Fri 9am-6pm, Sat-Sun 2pm-6pm. Admission charge. Tube: Monument

P20/21 St Paul's Cathedral, Ludgate Hill, EC4. ☎ 071 236 4128. Open Mon-Sat 9am-4.30pm. Whispering Gallery open Mon-Sat 9.45am-4.15pm. Crypt open Mon-Sat 8.45am-4.15pm. Admission charge. Tube: St Paul's.

P22/23 The Tower of London, Tower Hill, EC3. ☎ 071 709 0765. Open Mon-Sat 9.30am-5pm. Last admission 4pm. Admission Charge. Tube: Tower Hill.

Kathleen and May, St Mary Overy Dock, Cathedral Street, SE1. ☎ 071 403 3965. Open daily 10am-5pm. Admission charge. Tube: London Bridge.
HMS Belfast, Symon's Wharf, Vine Lane, SE1. ☎ 071 407 6434. Open daily 10am-5.30pm (summer), 10am-4.30pm (winter). Admission charge. Tube: London Bridge.
Tower Bridge, SE1. ☎ 071 403 3761. Open 10am-6.30pm (summer), 10am-4.45pm (winter). Admission charge. Tube: Tower Hill.
Cleopatra's Needle, Victoria Embankment. Tube: Embankment.

P26/27
St Paul's, Covent Garden, WC2. ☎ 071 836 5221. Tube: Covent Garden.
Royal Opera House, Bow Street, Covent Garden, WC2. ☎ 071 240 1200 for tours (group bookings only). Tube: Covent Garden
Theatre Royal, Drury Lane, Catherine Street, WC2. ☎ 071 836 3352 for tours (minimum 10 people).

P28/29
Trafalgar Day Parade, on nearest Sunday morning to Oct 21.
St Martin-in-the-Fields, Trafalgar Square, WC2. ☎ 071 930 0089. Tube: Charing Cross.
Norway Christmas Tree, set up in second week of December. Lights turned on by the Norwegian Ambassador. Carols sung every evening until Dec 25.

P30/31
Royal Mews, Buckingham Palace Road, SW1. ☎ 071 930 4832. Open Wednesdays 12am-4pm (Oct-March), Tues-Thurs 12am-4pm (March-Sept). Tube: Victoria.
Queen's Gallery, Buckingham Palace, SW1. ☎ 071 930 3007. Open Tue-Sat 10am-5pm. Sun 2pm-5pm. Tube: Victoria.
Changing of the Guard, Buckingham Palace, 11.30 am, daily in summer, alternate days in winter.

P32/33
St James's Park, SW1. Open 24 hours. Tube: St James's Park.
Green Park, SW1. Open 24 hours. Tube: Green Park.
Hyde Park, W.1. Open 5am-12pm. Tube: Hyde Park Corner.
Kensington Gardens, W1. Open 5am-dusk. Tube: Lancaster Gate.
Wellington Museum, Apsley House, 149 Piccadilly, W1. ☎ 071 499 5676. Open Tues-Sat 10am-5.50pm. Sun 2.30pm-5.50pm. Closed Jan 1, May Day, Good Friday, Dec 24-26. Admission charge. Tube: Hyde Park Corner.
Kensington Palace, the Broad Walk, Kensington Gardens, W8. ☎ 071 937 9561. Open Mon-Sat 9am-5pm. Sun 11am-5pm. Closed Jan 1, Good Friday, Dec 24-26. Admission charge. Tube: High Street Kensington.
London to Brighton Car Run — first Sunday in November, from Hyde Park Corner. Starts 7.30am.

P34/35
Regent's Park, NW1. Open 5am-dusk. Open-Air Theatre ☎ 071 486 2431. Open May-Sept. Tube: Regent's Park.
London Zoo, Regent's Park, NW1. ☎ 071 722 3333. Open 10am-5.30pm (March-Oct), 10am-4pm (Nov-Feb). Admission fee.
Alexandra Park, N22. Tube/BR: Wood Green
Battersea Park, SW11. BR: Battersea Park.
Blackheath, SE18. BR: Blackheath.
Clapham Common, SW4. Tube: Clapham Common
Crystal Palace Park, SE19. Open 8am-dusk. BR: Crystal Palace.
Hampstead Heath, NW3. Tube: Hampstead.
Holland Park, W14. Tube: Holland Park.

P36/37
British Museum, Great Russell Street, WC1. ☎ 071 636 1555, recorded information: ☎ 071 580 1788. Open Mon-Sat 10am-5pm. Sun 2.30pm-6pm. Closed Jan 1, Good Friday, May Day and Dec 24-27.

P38/39
Natural History Museum, Cromwell Road, SW7. ☎ 071 589 6323. Open Mon-Sat 10am-5.50pm. Sun 11am-5.50pm. Closed Jan 1, Good Friday, May Day and Dec 23-26. Tube: South Kensington

Geological Museum, Exhibition Road, SW7. ☎ 071 589 3444. Open Mon-Sat 10am-6pm. Sun 11am-6pm. Closed same as Nat.Hist.Museum. Tube: South Kensington.
Science Museum, Exhibition Road, SW7. ☎ 071 589 3444. Open Mon-Sat 10am-6pm. Sun 11am-6pm. Closed same as Nat.Hist.Museum. Tube: South Kensington.
V&A, Cromwell Road, SW7. ☎ 071 589 3456. Open Mon-Thurs & Sat 10am-5.50pm. Closed same as Nat.Hist.Museum. Tube: South Kensington.

P40/41
Madame Tussaud's and Planetarium, Marylebone Road, NW1 5LR. ☎ 071 935 6861, 071 486 1121. Open Mon-Fri 10am-5.30pm. Sat and Sun 9.30am-5.30pm. Admission charge. Tube: Baker Street.

Planetarium — shows daily from 10.20am-3.40pm.
Commonwealth Institute, Kensington High Street, W8 6NQ. ☎ 071 603 4535. Open Mon-Sat 10am-5pm. Sun 2pm-5pm. Closed Jan 1, Good Friday, May Day, Dec 24-26. Tube: High Street Kensington.
Museum of Mankind, 6 Burlington Gardens, W1X 2EX. ☎ 071 437 2224. Open Mon-Sat 10am-5pm. Sun 2.30pm-6pm. Closed Jan 1, Good Friday, May Day, Dec 25-27. Tube: Oxford Circus.

P42/43 **Hampton Court Palace**, East Molesey, Surrey. ☎ 081 781 9500. Grounds open dawn-dusk. Palace open Mon 10.15am-6pm and Tues-Sun 9.30am-6pm (Mar-Oct), Mon 10.15am-4.30pm and Tues-Sun 9.30am-4.30pm (Nov-Feb). Maze open same times as Palace. Closed Jan 1, Dec 24-26. BR: Hampton Court.

Richmond Park, Richmond, Surrey. ☎ 081 940 0654. Open March-Sept 7am-dusk, Oct-Feb 7.30am-dusk. BR/tube: Richmond.

Kew Gardens, Surrey. ☎ 081 940 1171. Open daily 9.30am-4pm. Sunday till 8pm. Closed Jan 1, Dec 25. Admission charge. Tube: Kew Gardens, BR: Kew Bridge.

P44/45 **National Maritime Museum**, Romney Road, SE10. ☎ 081 858 4422. Open Mon-Sat 10am-6pm, Sun 12am-6pm (summer). Mon-Sat 10am-5pm, Sun 2pm-5pm (winter). Closed Dec 24-26. Admission charge. BR: Greenwich.

Cutty Sark and Gipsy Moth IV, Greenwich Pier SE10. ☎ 071 858 3445. Open Mon-Sat 10.30-5.30 (summer), 10.30-4.30pm (winter). Sun and Good Friday from 12am. Closed Jan 1, Dec 24-26. Admission charge. BR: Greenwich.

Greenwich Park, SE10. Open from dawn till dusk. BR: Greenwich.

Thames Barrier Visitors' Centre, Woolwich. ☎ 081 854 1373. Open Mon-Fri 10.30am-5pm. Weekends 10.30am-5.30pm. Closed Jan 1, Dec 24-26. BR: Charlton.

Syon Park, Brentford, Middx. ☎ 081 560 0881-3. House open Wed-Sun 10am-6pm (April-Sep). Gardens open all year 10am-dusk. Closed Dec 25-26. Admission charge.

London Butterfly House, Syon Park. ☎ 081 560 7272. Open daily 10am-5pm (summer), 10am-3.30pm (winter).

Brit Koi Aquatic Centre, Syon Park. ☎ 081 847 4730. Open daily 9.30am-5.30pm (summer), 9.30am-5pm (winter). Admission charge.

Epping Forest Museum, Queen Elizabeth's Hunting Lodge, Rangers Road, Chingford, E4 7QH. ☎ 081 529 6681. Open Wed-Sun 2pm-6pm. BR: Chingford.

Whipsnade Park Zoo, Dunstable, Beds, LU6 2LF. ☎ 0582 872171. Open Mon-Sat 10am-6pm (summer), 10am-5pm (winter). Sun, Bank Hols till 7pm (dusk in winter). Closed Dec 25. Admission fee. BR: Luton, Bedford.

Chessington Zoo, Leatherhead Road, Chessington, Surrey. ☎ 0372 727227. Open daily 10am-5pm (summer), 10am-4pm (winter). Closed Dec 25. Admission fee. BR: Chessington South.

Windsor Castle, Windsor, Berkshire. ☎ 0753 868286. Castle precincts open 10am-dusk. State Apartments Mon-Sat 10.30am-5pm, Sun 1.30pm-5pm (May-Oct), Mon-Sat 10.30am-3pm (Nov-April). Closed June and when Royal Family are in residence. Admission charge. BR: Windsor and Eton.

P46/47 **Heathrow Airport**, Middlesex. ☎ 081 759 4321. Viewing deck open 10am-6pm. Admission charge. Tube: Heathrow Central.

Gatwick Airport, Sussex. ☎ Crawley (0293) 28822. Viewing deck open 9am-7pm. Admission charge. BR: Gatwick.

London Transport Museum, Covent Garden, WC2. ☎ 071 379 6344. Open daily 10am-6pm. Closed Dec 24-26. Admission charge. Tube: Covent Garden.

P48/49 **Harrods**, Knightsbridge, SWIX 7XL. ☎ 071 730 1234. Open Mon-Fri 9am-5pm. Wed 9.30am-7pm. Sat 9am-6pm. Tube: Knightsbridge.

Burlington Arcade, Piccadilly, W1. Closes 5.30pm and Sundays. Tube: Piccadilly.

Hamley's, 188-196 Regent Street, W1. ☎ 071 734 3161. Open Mon-Sat 9am-6pm, Thurs till 8pm. Tube: Oxford Circus, Piccadilly.

Liberty's, Regent Street, W1. ☎ 071 734 1234. Open Mon-Sat 9.30am-6pm, Thurs till 7.30pm. Tube: Oxford Circus, Piccadilly.

Fortnum & Mason, 181 Piccadilly, W1. ☎ 071 734 8040. Open Mon-Sat 9am-6pm. Tube: Piccadilly.

Billingsgate Market, Trafalgar Way, E14. Docklands Light Railway: West India Quay. BR: Stepney East.

New Covent Garden Market, Nine Elms, SW8. Tube: Vauxhall.

Smithfield Market, Charterhouse Street, EC1. Tube: Farringdon.

Spitalfields Market, Brushfield Street E1. Tube: Liverpool Street.

Brixton Market, Electric Avenue, SW9. BR: Brixton.

Leadenhall Market, Gracechurch Street, EC3. Tube: Bank.

Petticoat Lane, E1. Tube: Aldgate.

Portobello Road, W11. Tube: Notting Hill Gate.

P52/53 **Mounting the Queen's Guard**, Horse Guards Arch, SW1. Daily at 11am. Sun 10am.

Beating Retreat, Horse Guards Parade, SW1 (June only). Tickets from Ticket Centre, 1b Bridge Street, SW1. ☎ 071 839 6815.

Trooping the Colour, two rehearsals, plus ceremony at 11am on second Saturday in June. Tickets by ballot (two per person). Applications to: Brigade Major, Household Division, Horse Guards, Whitehall, SW1 – before Feb 1. Free first rehearsal only. ☎ 071 930 4466.

Beating the Bounds, around the Tower of London every third year (1993, 1996, 1999). Ascension Day, 11am. ☎ 071 709 0765 for details.

Pearly Harvest Festival,
St Martin-in-the-Fields, Trafalgar Square, WC2. ☎ 071 930 0089. First Sunday in Oct, 3.30pm.

Cart marking, Guildhall Yard. ☎ 071 606 3030 for details.

John Stow Memorial Service, St Andrew Undershaft, St Mary Axe, EC3. ☎ 071 283 7382 for details.

Lion Sermon, St Katherine Cree Church, Leadenhall Street, EC2. ☎ 071 283 5733 for details.

Pancake Greaze, Shrove Tuesday. Attendance by invitation of the Headmaster, Westminster School, Little Dean's Yard, SW1. Public pancake race at Lincoln's Inn Fields, WC2, at 11am.

Swan-Upping, crews set off from Temple Steps, Embankment, Monday 9.30am, third week of July.

Doggett's Coat and Badge Race, mid July, 11.15am from Tower Wharf. ☎ 071 626 3531.

Chinese New Year, celebrations in Gerrard Street, W1.

P54/55 **National Gallery,** Trafalgar Square, London, WC2N 5DN. ☎ 071 839 3321, recorded information: ☎ 071 839 3529. Open Mon-Sat 10am-6pm. Sun 2pm-6pm. Closed Jan 1, Good Friday, May Day, Dec 24-26. Tube: Charing Cross, Leicester Square, Piccadilly.

Tate Gallery, Millbank, London, SW1. ☎ 071 821 1313. Open Mon-Sat 10am-5.50pm. Sun 2pm-5.50pm. Closed Jan 1, Good Friday, May Day, Dec 24-26. Tube: Pimlico.

Royal Academy, Burlington House, Piccadilly, W1. ☎ 071 439 7438. Open daily 10am-6pm. Admission charge. Tube: Green Park, Piccadilly.

London Brass Rubbing Centre, St James's Church, 197 Piccadilly, W1. ☎ 071 437 6023. Open Mon-Sat 10am-6pm. Sun 12-6pm. Closed Dec 25-27. Charge for rubbings. Tube: St James.

Bethnal Green Museum of Childhood,

Cambridge Heath Road, E2 9PA. ☎ 071 980 2415. Open Mon-Thurs and Sat 10am-5.50pm. Sundays from 2.30pm. Closed Friday, Jan 1, May Day, Dec 24-26. Tube: Bethnal Green.

Molecule Theatre of Science for Children, 12 Mercer Street, London, WC2H 9QD. ☎ 071 379 5045 for details. Tube: Holborn

Polka Children's Theatre, 240 The Broadway, Wimbledon, London, SW19. Open Tues-Sat. ☎ 081 543 4888 or 071 543 0363 for details.

Unicorn Theatre for Children, 6-7 Great Newport Street, London, WC2H 7JB. ☎ 071 836 3334. Tube: Leicester Square.

The Little Angel Marionette Theatre, Dagmar Passage, Cross Street, Islington, London, N1 2DN. ☎ 071 226 1787 for details of performances. Tube: Angel or Highbury and Islington.

R.S.C., Barbican Centre, Silk Street, EC2. ☎ 071 628 3351 for tour details.

National Theatre, South Bank, SE1. ☎ 071 633 0880 for tour details.

Dickens' House, 48 Doughty Street, WC1. ☎ 071 405 2127. Open Mon-Sat 10am-5pm. Closed Bank Holidays and Dec 23-Jan 4. Admission charge. Tube: Russell Square.

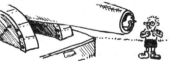

Extra Places to visit

Below is a list of some extra places to visit, not already mentioned in this book. Telephone to check admission times and prices before you go.

Cabinet War Rooms, Clive Steps, King Charles Street, London, SW1A 2AQ. ☎ 071 930 6961 or 071 416 5000. Underground emergency rooms for government during World War Two. Tube: Westminster.

Geffrye Museum, Kingsland Road, Shoreditch, E2 8EA. ☎ 071 739 9893. Exhibitions on English life since 1600. On Saturdays and in holiday times there are craft workshops for children. Tube: Liverpool Street.

Guinness World of Records, Trocadero Centre, Piccadilly Circus, W1. ☎ 071 439 7331. A model, video and computer display bring to life the amazing facts in the Guinness Book of Records. Tube: Piccadilly.

Imperial War Museum, Lambeth Road, London, SE1 6HZ. ☎ 071 416 5000. Displays on conflicts involving Britain and the Commonwealth since 1914. Tanks, aeroplanes, huge naval guns, weapons, uniforms, photos, films, sound effects and much more. Tube: Lambeth North, Elephant and Castle.

Kew Bridge Engines Trust, Green Dragon Lane, Kew Bridge Road, Brentford, Middx, TW8 OEN. ☎ 081 568 4757. A display of steam engines, including the largest working one in the world. The engines work at weekends. Tube: Gunnersbury.

London Dungeon, 28/34 Tooley Street, London, SE1 2SZ. ☎ 071 403 0606. Realistic tableaux of torture, disease and witchcraft in British history. Tube: London Bridge.

National Army Museum, Royal Hospital Road, SW3 4HT. ☎ 071 730 0717. Displays tell the story of the British Army from 1485. Holiday events for children such as model-making, quizzes and trying on original uniforms. Tube: Sloane Square.

Pollock's Toy and Theatre Museum, 1 Scala Street, W1. ☎ 071 636 3452. All kinds of toys including teddy bears and toy theatres. Tube: Goodge Street.

Royal Air Force, Battle of Britain and Bomber Command Museums, Grahame Park Way, Hendon, NW9. ☎ 071 205 2266. Three museums tracing the history of the RAF, the Battle of Britain campaign and the history of Bomber Command. Tube: Colindale.

City Farms

Below is a list of City Farms in the London area (see page 35).

Deen Farm, Batsworth Road, off Church Road, Mitcham, Surrey. ☎ 081 648 1461. Open Tue-Sun 9am-4pm. Weekends till 5pm.

Freightliners Farm, Paradise Park, Sheringham Road, N7 8PF. ☎ 071 609 0467. Open Tue-Sun 9.30am-5pm. Closed Dec 25-27.

Hackney City Farm, 1 Goldsmiths Row, London, E2. ☎ 071 729 6381. Open 10am-4.30pm, except Mondays. Closed Dec 25-27.

Kentish Town Farm, 1 Cressfield Close, NW5. ☎ 071 482 2861. Open Tue-Sun 9.30am-5.30pm.

Mudchute Community Farm, Pier Street, London, E14 9HP. ☎ 071 515 5901. Open 9am-5pm.

Brooks Farm, Skelton's Lane, Leyton, E10. ☎ 081 539 4278. Open Tue-Sun 10am-4pm.

Stepping Stones Farm, Stepney Way, London E1. ☎ 071 790 8204. Open 9.30am-1pm, 2pm-6pm, every day except Monday.

Surrey Docks Farm, South Wharf, Rotherhithe Street, SE16. ☎ 071 231 1010. Open 10am-5pm. Closed Fridays during school term.

Vauxhall City Farm, 24 St Oswald's Place, London SE11. ☎ 071 582 4204. Open 10.30am-5pm. Closed Mon and Fri. For more information about City Farms contact:

The National Federation of City Farms, AMF House, 93 Whitby Road, Brislington, Bristol, BS4 3QF. ☎ 0272 719109.

Crafts and drama

Below are some London arts centres and theatres that do special craft and activity classes for children.

Battersea Arts Centre, Lavender Hill, SW11. ☎ 071 223 8413. Lots of activities of all kinds on Saturday mornings and during school holidays.

Camden Arts Centre, Arkwright Road, NW3. ☎ 071 435 2643. Children's weekend and holiday classes.

Riverside Studios, Crisp Road, Hammersmith, W6 9RL. ☎ 081 748 3354.

Hall of Remembrance, Flood Street, SW3. ☎ 081 470 5802.

If you live in the London area your nearest library notice board is a good place for finding out about local activities.

River trips

Several companies run canal-boat trips along Regent's Canal. Services are usually during the summer months (April-Oct). Telephone for times and prices. Useful numbers are listed below.

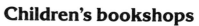

Zoo Waterbus ☎ 071 286 6101
London Waterbus Co. ☎ 071 482 2550
Jason's Canal Cruises ☎ 071 286 3428
Jenny Wren ☎ 071 485 4433
There are sightseeing boat Services along the Thames from Westminster, Charing Cross and Tower Piers. For details contact the
River Boat Information Service ☎ 071 730 4812

Bus trips

The following is a list of companies who run sightseeing bus tours around London. Contact them for details.

London Regional Transport – Details from tourist centres or any London Transport Travel Information Centre.
Big Bus ☎ 081 944 7810
Evan Evans ☎ 081 332 2912
London Cityrama ☎ 071 720 6663

Children's bookshops

Below is a list of children's bookshops in London. In addition many of the capital's general bookshops also have children's departments.

Women and Children First, 16 The Market, Greenwich, SE10. ☎ 081 853 1296.

Children's Book Centre, 237 Kensington High Street, London, W8. ☎ 071 937 7497.

Children's Bookshop (HMP Ltd), 29 Fortis Green Road, Muswell Hill, London, N10 3RT. ☎ 081 444 5500.

Puffins, 1 the Market, Covent Garden, WC2. ☎ 071 379 6465.

Free Walks

The Silver Jubilee Walk – a route stretching between Leicester Square and Tower Hill, marked by silver crown pavement plaques.

The London Wall Walk – a two-mile route laid out along the remains of Roman and medieval City Walls. It starts at the Museum of London, and ends at the Tower of London.

Yearly events

Below is a list of some extra yearly London events you can see.

February – Crufts Dog Show, Earls Court.
April – London Marathon, Greenwich Park to Westminster Bridge.
Easter Day (April) – Easter Parade (carnival procession and sideshows), Battersea Park.
Easter weekend – the International Model Railways Exhibition, Wembley Conference Centre.
Easter Monday (April) – Horse Harness Parade (gathering of London's working horses), Regent's Park Inner Circle.
May – Chelsea Flower Show, Royal Hospital, Chelsea.
June – Wimbledon Tennis Tournament, All England Lawn Tennis Club, Wimbledon.
June/July – Cricket Test Matches (England versus a touring team from Australia, India, West Indies, Pakistan or New Zealand), Lord's and the Oval cricket grounds.

July – Royal Tournament (military displays and competitions), Earls Court.
August – Notting Hill Carnival (street festival with Caribbean theme), Portobello Road area.

Cockney Rhyming slang

Cockney rhyming slang developed in Victorian times (see page 50), and some of its phrases are still used today. The way it works is simple – a word is substituted by a new word that rhymes with it. You might hear some of the examples below.

Loaf = head (loaf of bread)
Mince pies = eyes
North & South = mouth
Hampstead Heath = teeth
Dicky Dirt = shirt
Rosie Lee = tea
Tit for tat = hat
Whistle & flute = suit
Plates of meat = feet
Daisy roots = boots

Useful numbers

London Tourist Board, 26 Grosvenor Gardens, SW1. ☎ 071 730 3488. The Board runs information centres where you can buy sightseeing tickets and travel passes, and get free information on London in several languages. The main centre is outside Victoria Station. Open Mon-Fri 9am-6pm. Sat 9am-5pm. There are other centres at Heathrow, Selfridges (Oxford Street) and Harrods (Knightsbridge).

The City of London has its own information centre at St Paul's Churchyard, EC4. ☎ 071 606 3030

☎ **0839 123410** – a recorded message detailing monthly events in London.

☎ **0839 123424** – a recorded list of daily events in and around London especially for children.

☎ **071 222 8070** – Kidsline, a children's information service run by Capital Radio, listing events and activity suggestions. Open Mon-Fri 4pm-6pm during term-time, 9am-4pm during holidays.

Acknowledgements

The Publishers would like to thank the following organisations for permission to use references for illustrations in this book.

P6, Tower of London early layout, P11, Museum floor plan, Museum of London.
P14, Henry III with workmen at the Abbey, custody of the British Library, ref: cotton MS Nero D.i: ff 23v-24. Henry III's instructions to hurry work, custody of the Public Records Office, Close Roll (1252) : C54/65 m 32d.
P36/37, Trustees of the British Museum.
P38, Trustees of the British Museum (Natural History).
P39, Science Museum, Trustees of the V & A.
P41, Madame Tussaud's, Commonwealth Institute, Trustees of the British Museum.
P46, tube station picture based on 1925 poster by Chas W. Baker, Copyright London Transport Museum.

Index